Dan Latus lives in Northumberland with his wife. He grew up in Teeside, which has been his inspiration for this particular novel. Dan has also written *Never Look Back*.

RISKY MISSION

A mysterious young woman offers Frank Doy good money to drive her to a secret location in central Europe. And despite being warned off by her husband, Harry George — a dangerous Teesside gangster — Frank agrees to her request. But it's risky and the risks soon multiply. Mrs George is also taking along her two young children and a million pounds and Frank still has no idea where they are going. Meanwhile, Harry George wants — *needs* — his money back. But there's someone far more dangerous from his wife's past, who also has an interest in the money, and more . . .

Books by Dan Latus
Published by The House of Ulverscroft:

NEVER LOOK BACK

DAN LATUS

RISKY MISSION

Complete and Unabridged

ULVERSCROFT
Leicester

First published in Great Britain in 2011 by
Robert Hale Limited
London

First Large Print Edition
published 2012
by arrangement with
Robert Hale Limited
London

British Library CIP Data

Latus, Dan.
  Risky mission.
  1. Gangsters- -Fiction.
  2. Suspense fiction.
  3. Large type books.
  I. Title
  823.9′2–dc23

  ISBN 978–1–4448–1352–4

Published by
F. A. Thorpe (Publishing)
Anstey, Leicestershire

Set by Words & Graphics Ltd.
Anstey, Leicestershire
Printed and bound in Great Britain by
T. J. International Ltd., Padstow, Cornwall

This book is printed on acid-free paper

1

I don't always give him enough credit for it but sometimes Jimmy Mack is spot on with his forecasts. Like the time he said, 'I don't want to upset you, son, but this looks like trouble.'

I should have listened.

As it was, I broke off from what I was telling him and turned to see what he was staring at. It was a big four-wheel drive vehicle inching its way along the track from the main road.

'It looks more like money to me,' I told him.

He shook his head. 'Whenever a woman appears on the scene, there's terrible trouble close behind.'

I peered harder and realized he was right about the gender of the driver at least.

'You shouldn't be saying things like that, Jimmy, not in this day and age.'

He stared at me.

'It's sexist,' I explained. 'Politically incorrect. You can get done for it.'

He shook his head and gave me a pitying look. 'I don't know how you manage to stay in business,' he said mysteriously.

By then, the Isuzu Trooper had almost reached the parking area in front of my cottage.

'I'd better see what she wants,' I said.

Jimmy chortled and got back to mending his lobster pots. 'Go on, then,' he said, dismissing me. 'But don't make the mistake of asking her in, like you did the last one.'

'Sometimes,' I said carefully, 'I don't know what I've done to deserve a neighbour like you.'

'You must have gone to church when you were a young lad.'

'I don't think that's it,' I said, walking away.

I wasn't really complaining. Certainly not. There were just the two of us living at Risky Point, our glorious but isolated and retreating cliff top on the Cleveland coast, and I couldn't have hoped for a better neighbour than Jimmy Mack.

My cottage, the first one you came to along the track, was fifty yards or so from his. By the time I was halfway there, the newly arrived driver had opened the door and climbed out. She was young-ish, and tall and slim. She had long, dark hair, and she was wearing blue jeans and a white T-shirt. As soon as she felt the breeze coming off the sea, she reached back inside and brought out a leather jacket.

'Can I help you?' I called.

She shrugged into the jacket and turned to wait for me to reach her.

'Good morning,' she said. 'I am looking for Mr Doy, Mr Frank Doy. Do you know him?'

'That's me.'

She held out her hand, which I shook, but she didn't tell me her name.

'I would like to know if you can help me,' she said in careful, accented English. Obviously foreign. East European, I judged.

'I'll do my best,' I assured her. 'What is it you want?'

She didn't say anything more for a moment. She just stood there, unsmiling and considering. I wondered if I wasn't quite what she'd had in mind when she set off looking for help.

'I understand you run a private security service?' she said at last.

'That's right. I also do inquiries. Missing persons, crimes the police have given up on, insurance jobs.' I shrugged, smiled to reassure her and added, 'I do all sorts of things.'

'I understand.'

I wasn't sure she did. In fact, I thought she was probably wishing already that she had gone elsewhere.

'How many employees do you have?'

3

'Is that important?'

'Possibly.'

Oh, well. I knew then I wasn't going to get her business, whatever it was.

'There's just me,' I told her.

She had the cheek to look surprised. 'Just you?' she said. 'But I thought . . . '

'I bring in help, if it's needed.'

She stopped and looked around, fairly pointedly.

'But I'm usually enough,' I assured her gently.

'Yes?' She frowned. 'I thought you were president of a company.'

'Now who's been giving you that idea?'

She didn't answer. Looking worried, as well as cold, she wrapped her arms around herself and gazed out to sea.

I judged she was in her early thirties. But if she didn't stop worrying so much, she would soon look a lot older than that. Already I longed to see her smile.

'It's not very nice here,' she said, glancing at the cottage and managing not to shudder.

I don't mind admitting I was irritated by her comment. Affronted even. My cottage may be old and simple, but it means a lot to me. It had to, the work I'd put into it. Also, the views are stupendous. And you do get used to the wind.

So I found myself at a crossroads. Either I could disagree and wave her goodbye, or I could try to see it from her point of view.

'Would you like to come inside and tell me what you want over a cup of coffee?' I asked, hedging my bets.

She thought about it, sighed and nodded. 'Thank you,' she said.

*   *   *

At least she seemed to like the inside of the cottage. Her eyes darted everywhere, taking in the bare-board floor and the wooden ceiling, my rugs and the stone fireplace and chimney piece. Some of the solemnity left her face. I sensed a smile not too far away. Progress.

'It's very simple,' I pointed out.

'Yes,' she said. 'It is.'

My hopes sank again. Perhaps she didn't like it so much, after all.

'I know this type of house,' she added. 'It is a weekend cottage.'

'Not for me,' I told her. 'I live here all the time.'

'Oh?'

She seemed astonished. I didn't think the place was that bad.

'It's an old miner's cottage,' I added. 'I've

worked hard to improve it.'

'I can see that.'

She frowned, as if she was thinking the workmanship wasn't up to much. Then, surprisingly, she said, 'You have done well, I think.'

No doubt about it now. Definitely East European. I still didn't know what variety, though.

I got her sat down at the table in front of the window, and then I worked hard for a few minutes at heating water and making coffee.

'Normally,' I called from the other side of the big room that serves as both kitchen and living room, 'I would get the maid or the chef to do this, but it's their day off.'

'I don't like those people,' she muttered. 'Maids and chefs. I like to do such things myself.'

A rather odd comment. Not much sense of humour either. Not like mine anyway. I decided I would have to go easy on her.

'So,' I said, setting down two mugs of coffee at last, 'What's this all about? How can I help you?'

'No milk, thank you,' she said, moving the jug aside.

She poured in plenty of sugar, though, making me wonder if it was still rationed where she came from.

'You can drive a car?' she asked.

'Of course.'

'You have a driving licence and a passport?'

I nodded.

'Then I would like you to drive me somewhere.'

'Oh?'

'I will drive, too, but not so much, I think.'

I nodded again. She was a slow starter and I didn't want to interrupt her flow with questions.

'Yes?' she said.

'Yes. Sounds all right so far. Where do you want to go?'

'Somewhere far.'

'How far?'

'I can't tell you.'

Ah! That might be a problem.

'You don't know,' I said carefully, 'or you don't want to say?'

'Yes.'

It must be the language problem, I decided. So I sipped my coffee and stared out of the window. You couldn't see much of the sea from the living room — upstairs gave the best view — but I could see well enough to know there was a heavy fog hanging over the water still. There often is early in the day, but it was late morning now. The fog should have lifted.

There was fog on my brain, too.

'What do you think?' she asked.

'I think I need more information.'

'You want to know where we will go, yes?'

'That would be a good start.'

'I can't tell you,' she said again.

'No?'

She shook her head firmly.

'Well, tell me what you can tell me.'

She looked a little happier with that.

'This project will last two or three days for you. Maximum one week. Then you will return, alone, however you wish. For this, I will pay you £10,000. That is all. Thank you.

'What are you thinking?' she added in the silence that followed.

What I was thinking was it was a lot of money for a simple driving job. But I didn't say so. She might have lowered her offer.

'Is it somewhere in Europe?'

She hesitated and then nodded.

You could get a long way on European roads in a week. Macedonia? Northern Norway? The Urals? Further even.

'Is there anything else you can tell me?'

'What do you want to know?'

'When do you want to leave, for instance?'

'Tomorrow.'

That was a bit soon for me, but still . . . Ten grand could alter my timetable.

'Where from?'

'I will tell you when we start, if you come with me.'

Fair enough, I supposed.

'Anything else?' she asked.

'Why are you travelling? Why do you need someone like me? What's this about?'

She shook her head firmly. She wasn't going to say.

'OK. Here's the final question. Why me?'

'Because I heard you are a good man — poor, but good,' she added, glancing around my humble home-cum-business headquarters.

'You certainly know how to deliver a double-edged compliment,' I told her.

'Excuse me?'

I shook my head. 'It doesn't matter.'

But it did. Poor but good, eh? I was warming to her. Definitely. All the same, I wasn't sure I could sign up to driving somewhere I didn't know, somewhere quite possibly in a war zone. I was beginning to think Chechnya, Ingushetia, North Caucasus — good places like that.

So I asked her to let me think about it. I would call her and let her know.

'Today?'

'Today.'

She gave me her mobile number, but not

her name. I think she was disappointed I hadn't said yes on the spot. But that, I could have told her, is what you get when you proposition a good man, even one who's poor. You get lots of questions and prevarication.

2

I would have liked to help her, and the money was certainly good, but I didn't think I was going to do it. There were too many unknowns — and they were the ones I knew about.

Besides, so much money for such a small service was too good to be true. It smacked of something illegal or dangerous. Drugs or guns, for example. Perhaps both. Organized crime might come into it too. I wasn't prepared to take part in illegal trade, and I wasn't going to put myself in harm's way in a turf war either. Not just to help a pretty young woman who had started to intrigue me.

So I should have said no on the spot, just given her a straight answer, instead of saying I needed to think about it. But I didn't. No surprises there. One of my many failings is an inability to be crystal clear in my thinking and snappy in my decision taking. One or two people had told me that over the years. Especially women.

So I had told my visitor I would get back to her. After she left, I washed up and then went outside, where I sat at the picnic table I had long ago fashioned out of big lumps of driftwood and I listened to the sea eating the base of the cliffs. Once again, I wondered how long Jimmy Mack and I had got left here at Risky Point. Ours were the last two cottages remaining of the hamlet that once had adorned this cliff top, the rest taken by the sea. We were defying Nature.

That's where I was, and what I was doing, when Harry George rolled up in his flash car, an electric-blue Maserati. You don't see many of them at Risky Point.

Two visitors in one day? Three, if you counted his passenger. Jimmy Mack would be complaining about wear and tear on our jointly maintained access track.

A smart little guy climbed out from behind the wheel. It was a long time since my cottage had seen a suit as expensive as his, if ever, or an open-necked shirt as white. The wearer had glossy black hair and a tan that made you wonder where he'd been for his holiday. A big friendly smile, too. And he radiated energy.

His companion got out on the far side of the car and just stood there. I couldn't see much of him, but I could see enough to know that he wasn't smiling. He wasn't dressed as well either. A sallow-faced, mean-looking guy.

'Hi, there!' the little man called as he strolled towards me, hands in trouser pockets, jacket pushed back behind out of the way. 'How're you doing?'

'Pretty good,' I told him. 'Nice car,' I added.

'What, this?' He stopped, turned and gazed back at his machine fondly. 'I've never had better,' he admitted, turning back to me with a big grin.

'What does it do?'

'Top speed or fuel consumption?' He laughed and added, 'I don't think I want to tell you. You wouldn't believe me.'

'I might.'

'No.' He shook his head firmly. 'You wouldn't.'

'I'm Frank Doy,' I told him. 'Are you looking for me or for my neighbour, Jimmy Mack, over there in the other cottage?'

'You, I guess, Frank. Harry George, by the way.'

I nodded. He perched on a big rock nearby.

'Nice place you got here,' he offered, gazing at the cottage with apparent admiration. 'Isn't it, Leroy?' he added, turning to his sidekick.

Leroy nodded without looking. He stayed behind the car, staring at me.

'It suits me,' I said.

'That's what counts.'

So, Harry George. With that surname and those looks, he had to be Greek. Some way back, though. A generation or two, perhaps; he had a Teesside accent. But his style was more Miami Beach than Middlesbrough, still less Thessalonika.

Nice and easy did it, I decided. It's hard to dislike someone working so hard at being friends. I was trying, though. He was too familiar for my taste.

As for Leroy, well . . . I'd seen his like before. A nasty bastard. The greying hair didn't fool me. Slight of build, whipcord tough, eyes like a weasel. He wasn't muscle; he was a knife man, and he looked as mean and sharp as they come.

That placed Happy Harry for me, too. Time they were both on their way.

'What can I do for you, Harry?'

'You do interesting work for a living, Frank. I've been asking around,' he added when I raised my eyebrows.

'Interesting?' I mused. 'Not particularly. Not often, anyway. Usually it's pretty boring.'

'Security work, investigations . . . ? Sounds interesting to me.'

'I only do it for the money,' I told him. 'It's not a vocation.'

'So if you won the Lottery tomorrow, you would — '

14

'Sail off into the sunset. Damn right, I would.'

Actually, I wouldn't. I would stop right here and fix my cottage up properly. Try to stop it falling into the sea. Sort the garden out. Get a decent car. Pursue Lydia more earnestly, maybe. Do some serious fishing. But I wasn't going to admit any of that to Harry George.

'I could use some extra security,' he said.

'Oh?'

He pulled out a couple of small cigars, cheroots, from his inside jacket pocket and offered me one. I shook my head. He lit his. A dense grey cloud lifted up into the sunshine. The stench was nauseating.

'I'm in business, Frank, and one or two of my places get broken into pretty regularly.'

'What sort of places?'

'Industrial units. And clubs, night spots. I could do with hiring someone to take overall charge of security.'

Even if I'd liked him, it wasn't a job for me. I could go in and structure it for him but I didn't need an employer. That wasn't how I worked.

I didn't say so at the outset, though. Caution inhibited me. I felt he still had more to say. And I'm good at letting people take their time, and tell me in their own way.

'Frank, I understand my wife came to see you this morning.'

'Oh?'

'Can you confirm that?'

'I can't, no.'

'Can't or won't?' he asked with a little chuckle.

A warning bell began to jingle softly.

'Harry, what is it you want? Did you come here to offer me a job, or what?'

'I came to find out what my wife said to you this morning, Frank. But there might be a job in it for you, as well, if you play your cards right.'

'Thanks very much. I'll think about it and let you know.'

'Let me know what?'

'If I want the job.'

He smiled. Then he laughed. 'And my wife?' he said.

'Never heard of her. What did you say her name was again? Mrs . . . George, was it?'

He stopped laughing. He didn't even smile any more. 'Frank,' he said, 'this isn't funny.'

'You're right. It isn't.'

'I know she came to see you. All I want to know from you is what she came to see you about. That's not too much to ask, is it?'

You had to admire the cheek and self-confidence of the guy, but not enough for

16

me to want to betray a potential client's confidence. I wasn't even prepared to admit anyone had been here. But I had a fair idea now who my visitor had been.

'I get no end of women here,' I told him. 'Jimmy Mack's always complaining about them. You can't expect me to remember if one of them was your wife.'

'She came this morning.'

'What does she look like?'

'Tall, long dark hair . . . ' He stopped, smiled again and added, 'Don't fuck with me, Frank.'

'I think it's time you left,' I told him. 'I don't like your attitude. And whatever the job is, I'm not interested anyway.'

Out of the corner of my eye I saw Leroy come out from behind the car. I held up my hand and told him, 'That's far enough! Any closer and I stop being polite.'

For emphasis I picked up a length of two-by-four that happened to be lying nearby.

'Whoa, gentlemen!' Harry said.

Leroy stood still.

'Fair enough.' Harry had recovered and was back to smiling again. 'You're not going to work for me, Frank, and you sure as hell aren't going to work for her either.'

He really was beginning to irritate me but I just stared at him, believing he would get the message eventually.

'Let me tell you about her,' he said. 'She's crazy. She does stupid things, says stupid things. Thinks them, as well.'

'Yeah?'

'Yeah. And she's dangerous. Especially to someone like you, Frank, she's dangerous. She could get your house burned down. Maybe even get you killed. Have nothing to do with her. That's my advice to you, Frank. Follow my advice, and we'll forget this little disagreement.'

'That's good to know,' I said, keeping half an eye on Leroy, wanting to be ready if he started moving again.

'Isn't it?' Harry smirked and added, 'But ignore my advice, Frank, and you'll be in trouble — big trouble.'

It was beginning to sound like he was auditioning for a part in one of Scorsese's movies. He looked the part, too, with the Maserati and his suntan and suit and all. But he hadn't quite got it right.

'You'll have to work on the accent,' I told him, shaking my head.

'What?'

'It sounds more Middlesbrough than Vegas or Brooklyn. You want to take lessons. Find yourself a good voice coach, if you're serious about making this movie.'

'The fuck you're talking about?'

He glowered at me for a moment and then got to his feet abruptly, as if he couldn't abide madness. 'Just remember what I told you!' he snapped.

Then he turned and strode off to his fancy car. Leroy followed close behind. I guessed Harry was pretty mad by then. Some people don't like being laughed at.

'If you ever think of selling that thing,' I called after him, 'be sure to let me know. I'll make you a good offer.'

I nearly added that I wished him luck in the search for his wife, but thought better of it. He'd already given me much to think about. I didn't need him coming back at me with an automatic weapon doing his talking.

I didn't need to see anything more of Leroy either. I smiled at him pleasantly as he gave me a last glower before stooping to follow his boss back into the car.

'Nice meeting you, Leroy. You, too, Harry!'

As they bucketed along the track at unreasonable speed, heads no doubt banging on the roof every time they hit one of the many potholes, I regretted the offer I'd made on the car. It wasn't going to be up to much by the time Harry was finished with it.

I wasn't in such a happy mood as I'd made out either. I'd seen enough trouble in my life to recognize it when it came calling.

So she was Harry's wife, was she, my mysterious visitor? That changed things. Even if I hadn't been very taken with her at the time, I would have been better disposed towards her now. I wondered more than ever what she had in mind.

★ ★ ★

I rang her ten minutes later.

'I'd like to accept your offer,' I told her.

'Yes?'

'Yes. So what happens next?'

'I will collect you from your house. Please have with you your passport and driving licence and personal things for a few days.'

'OK. When?'

'Nine o'clock tomorrow morning.'

'Fine. There's one thing you should know.'

'Yes?'

'A man claiming to be your husband, a Harry George, has just been to see me. He wanted to know what you said to me.'

That jolted her. There was a long pause.

'He must have had me followed,' she said eventually. 'What did you tell him?'

'Nothing. I said I didn't know his wife.'

'And he accepted that?'

'Not really. He sort of threatened me.'

'He would. That is his way. Mr Doy,' she added, 'is that why you have said yes to me?'

'Probably.'

'Then I have chosen the right man to help me.'

She rang off then, leaving me with a self-righteous glow.

3

I rang a cop friend, Bill Peart. He was a detective inspector, at the time, based in Middlesbrough.

'Bill, do you know anything about a tough guy called Harry George? Claims to be some sort of businessman. Over your way, probably.'

'Your way, as well, Frank. That's Harry the Greek. He owns clubs, amongst other things. One of them's in Redcar. *Aphrodite's?*'

Ah! I should have known.

Then I smiled. Harry the Greek! Cops, eh?

'That's his, is it? The locals just call it 'The Greek's'.'

'Not surprising, is it? What do you want to know about him?'

'What have you got? He's just offered me a job.'

Bill chuckled. 'Tell me you didn't take it!'

'You know me, Bill. I'll do almost anything if the money's right.'

'The money will never be right in this case. He's a nasty piece of work.'

'What have you got on him?'

'Nothing much — yet. But he's in the

frame for most things: drugs, prostitution, violence. It's just a matter of time before we take him off the streets.'

That was Bill being optimistic again. I hoped his optimism was justified.

'A guy called Leroy rides with him.'

'That's right. He's a serious piece of work, as well. Does a lot of the heavy stuff himself because he likes it.'

'A killer?'

'Very likely. We'll get him eventually. We'll get them both — and the rest.'

'Thanks, Bill. I don't think I'll take the job, after all.'

'You're welcome!' he said with an undisguised chuckle. 'Let me know when the fishing's good, Frank. I'll come down and see you again.'

* * *

I was ready early the next morning. I wasn't taking much with me and my gear was packed in a bag sitting next to the front door. I was ready, but she didn't show up.

I hung around the kitchen for a while. Then I went outside and peered along the track. Nothing. By 9.30 I knew she wasn't coming. Either she had changed her mind or Harry George had changed it for her.

It was a pity. I'd been looking forward to a foreign trip, and a long drive in a decent vehicle on decent roads. The ten grand would have come in handy, too. I could have fixed the roof properly with that. Maybe stabilized the cliff, as well. But I should have known it was too good to be true. All I could do was hope the lady had survived the indiscretion of coming to see me.

My thoughts turned to matters closer to home. It was shaping up to be a grand day. Our cottages, mine and Jimmy Mack's, have a fine cliff-top location. As I looked out over the bay I could see that the thin, cold mist was soon going to be burned off by the sun. Then one of those glorious May days would follow: blue sky and heat. And at this time of year the tide would be high, and perhaps spectacular. Already the sea was starting to roar as it began its drive for the base of the cliffs. So there were worse places to be than this, if your foreign holiday fell through.

I wandered over to the edge of the cliff and then down the barely existent path to the beach. The fish would be jumping in surf like this. Maybe I would get the rod out later and do a bit of fishing from the beach. It had been a while since I'd done that but Bill Peart had put the possibility in mind. I might see if Jimmy Mack wanted to come down with me.

He didn't do so much fishing these days. He was feeling his age. But it was still in his blood. It was what he had done all his life, as had umpteen generations of Macks before him.

The breeze and the sound and scent of the sea put me in a good frame of mind. When I climbed back to the top of the cliff it was almost a disappointment to see that the putative Mrs George had turned up after all. The big four-wheel drive was standing next to the cottage, and she was sitting inside it. I gave her a wave but she didn't respond.

'You should have been here!' she accused when I reached the car.

'I was,' I told her. 'But I decided you weren't coming. I thought you must have changed your mind.'

By then, I was looking hard at her. I had been about to point out she was very late but I could see now she had done well to get here at all.

'You all right?'

She nodded but she didn't look it.

'Come inside for a bit.'

'No!' She straightened up abruptly. 'No, thank you. We must go — quickly. Please,' she added.

'We're still going?'

'Yes, yes! We must. Now he knows about

you, he will come here. If he finds me, it will be bad for us all.'

Harry George, she presumably meant.

'He really is your husband?'

She nodded.

'And he did this to you?'

'Yes.'

Her eyes were narrow slits in a swollen face. She looked like she had been in a car crash, or a game of rugby.

'You sure you want to go ahead with this? Maybe you should go to the police instead.'

'I am sure,' she said. 'Please. We must hurry.'

For a moment I wasn't sure what to do or say. But she was right about one thing: Harry George would certainly come here looking for her. I collected my bag. We could sort things out when we were on the road.

Another surprise awaited me when I returned to the car. Two little people had appeared on the back seat.

'Hello!' they chorused, giggling and clearly delighted to have surprised me.

'Who are you?' I asked with astonishment.

'I'm Hannah,' said the one with long blonde hair. 'And that's Petr,' she said, pointing to the one with short blond hair.

'My children,' added the one in the front seat with long dark hair.

'I guessed.'

I hesitated, wondering about this enormous complication. But she had moved over to vacate the driver's seat for me. So I occupied it and glanced at the controls.

Compared with what I was used to driving, this looked like an executive jet — lights and dials everywhere. But my mind was only half on the controls. I was also busy trying to work out what I had let myself in for. I decided to defer talking about it until we were moving. That might be safer.

'Which way?' I asked as we trundled down the track.

'Head west on the A174.'

'Towards Middlesbrough?'

'Yes.'

OK. She was being cautious. Walls have ears, as they used to say, even inside cars. I didn't press her. I just wanted to get the show on the road. She had obviously had a rough morning.

I turned off gravel and on to tarmac, and moved up to a sensible speed. I was interested in seeing how this vast assemblage of metal and plastic was going to handle on a normal road. Quite well, was my early feeling.

'So the passengers are Hannah and Petr,' I began, 'and I'm Frank. You are?'

She didn't answer immediately.

'It could be a long trip, Mrs George,' I pointed out.

'Vlasta. My name is Vlasta.'

'Thank you. So how are you feeling, Vlasta? Any injuries I can't see?'

She shrugged, and immediately regretted it. 'Not many. He likes to make his punishments visible,' she said when the pain had subsided.

Nice. So friendly Harry was one of them, was he? And there was me thinking wife beating had gone out of fashion.

'Punishments? What for?'

'This time for visiting you.'

That hurt. I wished I'd planted one on him while I'd had the chance.

'What did you tell him about our meeting?'

'At first, nothing. Then I told him I went to see you because I would like a dog. The children would like a dog,' she amended.

I had to smile. 'Did he buy that?'

'Not really, but he was in a hurry and didn't have much time to waste on me.'

Harry seemed to have used what little time he had very effectively, judging by her appearance.

'So I'm a dog trader, am I?'

'I told him my friend said you knew about dogs.'

'So why did he have a problem with that?'

'He doesn't like dogs.'

'No?'

'They make a mess everywhere and they make his eyes water. He is . . . What do you say?'

There were a few names I could have suggested. Instead, I said, 'Allergic?'

'Yes. Allergic.'

'So he beat you up because you were thinking about getting a dog?'

'Yes. For me, it was good. If he knew what I was really thinking and doing, he would kill me.'

So she was tough and smart. Prepared to accept looking as if she had been hit by a bus in order to achieve something important to her, whatever that was.

'You've left him, I take it?'

'Yes.'

'And taken the kids?'

She didn't admit that part of the obvious.

'He may take it badly.'

'He said he would kill me if it ever happened.'

'And you believe he will try?'

'Oh, yes. He has killed other people, I think. He will not hesitate.'

Her answer gave me plenty to think about. At least now, though, I had some idea what I had got myself into. Quite a lot, it seemed.

'OK,' I said.

'Excuse me?'

'I said it's OK. I will do what I said.'

'Thank you.'

It didn't seem to have occurred to her that any normal, reasonably intelligent man would by now have returned her money and boarded a bus back home.

'Where does he think you are now, Vlasta?'

'I took the children to school, he thinks.'

So we had a bit of time before he realized she'd fled. We would need to use it well.

'And where are we going now?'

'You will see.'

I left it at that until we hit the A19. Then I had to raise the subject again.

'Left or right?' I asked. 'North or south?'

'South,' she told me reluctantly.

Even more reluctantly, she added, 'We go to Hull. Do you know this place?'

'Yes. Presumably the ferry terminal?'

'Yes.'

She curled up then and left me to it. I wondered if her injuries were only superficial. I certainly hoped so.

The kids were curled up, too, as if they had been hauled out of bed in the middle of the night and needed to catch up on their sleep. Some life, they all seemed to lead, the George family.

* * *

It was about a two-hour drive to Hull. Maybe it would have been quicker if we had cut straight south from my place. On the other hand, I could understand Vlasta's thinking; there was greater anonymity on busier roads, and perhaps less chance of being followed. We stopped at the Ferrybridge motorway service centre, where the A1 and M62 intersect, to stretch our legs. Vlasta was on edge and urged the kids to hurry when they went to the washrooms.

'Are you worried about being followed?' I asked her.

'Harry will not give up.'

'He won't know where we are.'

She appeared unconvinced.

'Will he know you're leaving the country?'

She shrugged. 'Perhaps. There is nowhere in England I can go.'

'Where are you from, Vlasta?'

She shook her head, declining to answer.

'It would be nice to know where we're going,' I pressed gently.

'You will, eventually.'

But not yet, it seemed.

The kids returned and I got the show back on the road.

I wondered if the kids knew what was

happening. Quite possibly, they thought they were going on holiday, but somehow I doubted it. For a start, they had me rather than Daddy to drive them. But they might well be used to the idea they couldn't play happy families. What Daddy had done to Mummy that morning wouldn't have been a one-off event. For all that, they were pretty good kids, seemingly resilient and pleasantly sensible. I hoped I could help them all.

'Hannah, are you warm enough, back there?' I called.

'Yes, thank you. We have travel rugs for if we are cold.'

'That's good. And you have things to do?'

'I like to look out of the window. Petr likes to sleep.'

I couldn't help smiling. She was like a little old lady. I smiled across at Vlasta, who did her best to smile back. 'They're nice children,' I said.

'Thank you.'

'How do you feel?' I added, wondering if she needed anything. A hospital, maybe? At least a doctor.

'I have felt better.'

'Have you taken anything for the pain?'

'No.'

'I have some painkillers in my bag. Do you want one?'

'No, thank you. No drugs.'

But my question had alerted her to her appearance. She dug into her bag and began to apply make-up. The cosmetic repair work was sensible. Otherwise we might not be allowed on to the ferry. That would be a fine start: me arrested on suspicion of domestic violence.

'Is that better?' she asked.

I nodded.

But only on the surface was it better. I knew that much.

4

Harry was in a dangerous mood. Leroy recognized the signs as they sped off from Risky Point. Harry swore softly and repeatedly. He took the Maserati into tight corners at ridiculous speed, and came out the other side still intact. Then he looked eagerly for the next challenging bend and went into it even faster. In his own mind, Leroy likened their progress to Russian Roulette. He didn't care for it. There were other ways.

'What do you want to do?' Leroy said eventually.

'What about?' Harry snapped.

'The guy. Him and your wife.'

'There's no him and my wife! Got that? He's a nobody. Thinks he's a private eye, that's all.' Harry snorted with derision. 'And her! Well . . . ' he concluded, words failing him.

'So what do you want to do?'

'She's going to tell me what I want to know. She won't want to, but she will. Then we'll see.'

To Leroy, nobody got away with messing with the boss's wife. There could be only one answer to that. 'And the guy?' he said. 'Waste him?'

'Not yet.'

Harry frowned and slowed down. That pleased Leroy. It meant the boss was thinking again. They might survive the journey after all.

Harry added, 'It might come to that.'

'Just say the word,' Leroy said, settling deeper into his bucket seat. 'I didn't like the sonovabitch.'

'Might burn his house down first,' Harry said with a sly sideways grin. 'See what he thinks about that.'

Leroy nodded appreciatively. 'That would get him going. He seemed to like his house a lot.'

'Yeah,' Harry said. 'You could tell.'

'Burn his house down. Then waste him,' Leroy said with a smile. 'That's some plan, boss.'

Harry nodded and concentrated again on his driving. He really liked this car. And so far as he could see, things were working out fine. He was going to come out ahead after all. Vlasta ought to be able to see that. If she couldn't, he could do without her. More trouble lately than she was worth.

5

We were to travel on the P&O Hull-Zeebrugge ferry, the *Pride of York*. My client decided to tell me that much as we drove into Hull. Boarding time closed at 7.30 p.m.; sailing time was nine o'clock. We were in good time, arriving soon after four to join the queue of cars already waiting to be let on board.

'What are the arrangements?' I asked.

'Arrangements?'

'How are we to travel?'

'We have a cabin. We sail at nine.'

Still very much the need-to-know principle in action. I couldn't blame her, not now I'd seen her face both before and after Harry had worked on it. She had no reason to trust anyone but herself.

'One cabin?'

'Yes. A cabin for four people.'

That was good. I was relieved there was no silliness like putting me in a separate cabin. This wasn't just a driving job. I needed to be close at all times if I was going to earn my money.

'Will we have bunk beds?' Hannah asked.

36

'Yes,' her mother said.

'Can I have a top one?'

'If you like.'

'Bunk beds?' Petr said. 'On a ship?'

It was left to Hannah to explain. I noted that English wasn't the language in which she chose to do it.

Vlasta was hyper. Her eyes were everywhere, and even though she had been well in control until now I sensed she was running on the energy that comes with fear.

'Hey!' I said softly, giving her a smile. 'Calm down. Nothing's going to happen here. Not on my watch.'

'You don't know him,' she pointed out, but at least she gave me a token smile back.

Then she got on her mobile. Whoever she spoke to, the conversation was brief, and not in English.

I let it go. When we were into the journey proper she would have to tell me more. I would insist on it. For now, I had enough to think about.

A lot of what I was thinking was that a ship can be a dangerous place, a trap even. Once aboard, you're there for the duration. There's no getting off early, not alive. I would have to be vigilant. Harry probably wouldn't try anything while we were at sea, but he might.

It didn't have to be Harry in person either. With all his resources, he would be able to call on more than Leroy if he needed to. That thought gave me more to ponder. I'd got into this easily enough but the road ahead might prove hard to leave.

We sat there for twenty minutes. Then the queue came to life and vehicles surged forward, up the ramp and into the bowels of the *Pride of York*. In the gloom of the hold, I switched on the lights and followed the car ahead of me in a loop that led us to a place alongside a line of motor homes. On the other side of that was a line of trucks. Yellow-jacketed figures waved me on until one of them brought us to a stop a yard behind the car in front. It didn't feel like a good place to be.

People were spilling out of their cars, rummaging in boots and on back seats, coming away with bags, rugs, coats. Seasoned travellers, perhaps. Knowing what to expect. Vlasta was one of them.

'What do you need to take?' I asked as she opened her door and prepared to climb out.

'We have everything ready,' she said over her shoulder.

I opened the tailgate. Vlasta took out a small holdall; the kids picked up backpacks. I shrugged and reached for my own bag. I hoped they were always so well prepared.

Then I paused, unable to believe my eyes. Another bag, a big holdall, was partially unzipped. I stared hard for a moment at what I could see of the contents. Then I pulled the zip across to close the bag.

I stepped back and reached up to pull the rear door down. I slammed it shut and locked the vehicle with the remote. Then I turned to the others, who were waiting more or less patiently. Vlasta seemed unaware of what I'd seen and I tried not to give her a hint.

'Let's go,' I said.

We studied the number on the nearest door to the stairwell, and the deck number on the wall inside. Then we told each other we must remember them and set off up the stairs, like everyone else. But in other ways we were almost certainly unlike anyone else at all on that ship.

The situation seemed even more complicated, and dangerous, now. Harry George was going to discover it wasn't only his wife and kids that were missing. Perhaps he already had.

As for me, I was troubled by the knowledge that I'd never seen so much money, not in one place.

★　★　★

The kids soon adjusted to life aboard ship. In fact, they were so pleased with the bunks they wanted to go to bed straight away. Vlasta said no.

'They go to bed now,' she told me, 'and in one, two hours they will want to get up again. Then where will we be?'

Where indeed. Vlasta was an omniscient mother.

Soon after nine the captain announced over the tannoy that loading was complete and we were about to make a start. It seemed a good time to venture up on deck and watch the laborious process by which the *Pride of York* inched its way out of the King George V dock, through the lock and out into the Humber. There was perhaps a foot to spare each side of the ship as we squeezed our way through the lock. It was no time or place for learner drivers on the bridge.

I smiled at Vlasta, straightened up and turned round, prepared to trust the captain. A small crowd milled around the rear deck, where we stood. People were torn between marvelling at the seamanship involved and their last sight of Hull. I caught the eye of a man with binoculars slung round his neck who appeared to be doing neither. He was, if anything, looking at me. Vlasta said something that required my attention. When I

40

looked round again the man was gone.

It was nothing, nothing at all. Yet it served as a wake-up call. I wasn't here just for the ride. It was entirely possible that Harry could have placed somebody, if not himself, aboard the *Pride of York*. I needed to be on guard.

When the ship was well out in the Humber I suggested to Vlasta that we should find the restaurant. She seemed dubious about that.

'We have to eat,' I insisted. 'Better to do it now and get it out of the way before it's dark.'

She nodded and summoned Hannah and Petr.

Near the doorway I saw the man with binoculars again. He was busy cleaning the lenses.

★　★　★

The kids had been remarkably restrained about my presence so far. Presumably, Vlasta had said something to them that covered it. But over dinner Hannah began to fish, and in the process, to betray things her mother would no doubt have preferred to keep secret.

'Frank,' she said, toying with her chips, 'are you coming with us to see Grandmother and Grandfather?'

'I'm not sure.'

'It would be nice. They live — '

'Hannah!' Vlasta warned.

That ended that line of conversation, for the moment. I was left to reflect. It would make some sort of sense, I supposed, to take the children and go home to Mother. The trouble was that Harry could probably see that, too.

I glanced at Vlasta and smiled to reassure her that I wasn't trying to prise out information she wasn't ready to divulge. 'Sooner or later, though,' I murmured, 'I will need to know more.'

'Soon,' she said. 'I will tell you soon.'

OK. I could wait a little longer. While we were at sea, I didn't really need to know much more. And I could always try not to speculate about the money.

My guess now was that we were headed for somewhere in the heart of Europe. The language I had heard them using was not one I knew. Not Scandinavian or German. Not a Romance language either. More eastern European. Slavonic probably, but it didn't have the drone of Russian or Polish.

I didn't know what the hell it was. There were so many countries and languages out there. All those territories that used to be part of the Soviet Union and its empire. The language could easily be one I'd never even heard of.

On the way out of the restaurant I saw the man with the binoculars again. My impression was that he was trying hard not to look at me. That stirred my interest. He was a nondescript, wiry sort of guy heading for middle age. Perfect for the role of watcher. But I could do watching, too.

★   ★   ★

The cabin we shared was small but adequate. It had its own tiny bathroom — smaller than the proverbial broom cupboard — and two sets of bunk beds. It had almost everything you could have wanted, in fact, except a window with a sea view. That deficiency made it a bit claustrophobic. It wasn't a place where we could easily spend the next few hours before bedtime. So I wasn't surprised that the kids soon exhausted the play potential of the bunk beds and wanted to explore further afield.

'Can we go round the ship?' Hannah asked.

Vlasta glanced at me. I nodded. If Harry did have someone aboard the ship, that would mean he already knew we were here. We wouldn't be giving anything away. In any case, nothing was going to happen soon, if at all. Now wasn't the time to be snatching the children or beating up Vlasta again.

'I don't see why not,' I told her, 'as long as we keep inside, and don't go out on deck.'

No point taking unnecessary risks, especially at night.

There was plenty to see, and to hear. We found a pop group performing in the disco area, and a dinner-jacketed pianist in the more rarefied atmosphere of the Piano Lounge. Hannah seemed particularly interested in the casino operation but I steered her away from that and we settled in a quiet corner with a big TV and non-stop Sky News. We might have been a happy little family from some decent suburb heading for a much-deserved holiday. If only!

Vlasta was quiet. Subdued even. Understandably so; she had a lot on her mind. I wondered how far ahead her planning had gone. Better not to ask, I decided. There was always the possibility that all her energy and thinking had gone into getting us to here, and that now she was away from Harry she didn't know any more than I did what came next.

I went for more coffee for me and a couple of cokes for the kids. Vlasta didn't want anything. When I returned to our table Vlasta wasn't there. Hannah said she had gone to the washroom. I hoped she would be able to do something more about her face. The bruises were looking ugly again as they darkened. I didn't want them to attract attention.

Petr was looking unhappy now. I wondered if it was seasickness but he shook his head when I asked him. He just sat and stared at his coke without touching it. The stress, I decided. Not surprisingly, it was getting to him too.

Hannah was fine, though. She was having a good look around, as well as enjoying her coke. She was particularly interested in what the young women were wearing, which in some cases wasn't very much at all.

'Petr,' I said, 'would you like something else to drink, instead of the coke?'

He shook his head and, all credit to him, made a big effort to look less miserable. It didn't work.

'He likes a straw,' Hannah said.

'What?'

'A straw — to drink with.'

The penny dropped, as it probably would have done a lot earlier with any dad. I returned to the service area and claimed a couple of straws. Petr's eyes lit up when I dumped the straws in his glass. His smile said it all. Now he was happy!

Nice kid, I thought. They both were. Rotten father, but nice kids. It said a lot for Vlasta.

'Where's Mum?' Hannah asked, putting a stop to my sentimental reverie. 'Do you know?'

I didn't.

★ ★ ★

She wasn't back yet. I looked around but couldn't see her. I began to worry.

The lounge was filling up now and the pianist was playing his heart out. At least, I thought so until I glanced his way. Then I saw he wasn't even there — the piano was playing itself. I nudged Hannah and pointed, to take her mind off the question I couldn't answer.

She giggled. 'The Invisible Man?' she suggested.

'It must be. Can you stay right here and look after Petr for a minute, Hannah? I want to find your mum.'

'Of course. Are you worried about her?'

'A little. She might not be feeling well. Some people don't like being at sea.'

She nodded and said something to Petr that was unintelligible to me. He nodded, too.

I didn't want to go far from the kids but I was uneasy about Vlasta. She had been gone ten, fifteen minutes.

The lounge was horseshoe-shaped, and part of it couldn't be seen from where we were sitting. Vlasta wasn't in that part. She wasn't in the general area outside the lounge either, the area where the Info Desk was. I hesitated. She might still be in the ladies, but which one? She might also have returned to the cabin, but without saying anything? It didn't seem very likely. I grimaced with frustration.

Then I saw her through a window. She was outside, on the narrow deck that ran along the side of the ship. Light fell on her face as someone opened a door.

I pushed through the double doors that led on to the deck. For a moment, I paused, surprised. She was talking to the man with the binoculars.

'Vlasta?'

They both looked round. She seemed OK. I was relieved. The man said something. She nodded. Then he turned and walked away. She began moving towards me.

'How are you feeling?' I asked her.

'Better, thank you. I needed some air.'

'Who was he?'

'Just another passenger.'

I hesitated but in the end kept quiet. Yes, I had seen him several times, but that wasn't surprising. It was a passenger ship. And people, travellers, did speak to each other.

So we went back inside and sat a while

longer. I was watchful but we seemed safe enough for the moment. The kids were happy, their eyes flitting between TV and the youngsters passing by. Vlasta wasn't happy, though. That wasn't a surprise. Her bruising would be uncomfortable, not even thinking of any damage I couldn't see. Also, she had a lot on her mind — and plenty to worry about. I wondered once again what the plan was, but didn't ask. I was tired of asking.

Vlasta announced that she was going to the duty-free shop.

'Want me to go for you?' I asked.

She shook her head. 'I need to move,' she said.

Hannah was interested, too, but she was also rebuffed. Vlasta went alone.

The rest of us watched TV as Sky News came around for the umpteenth time, showing US troops on the streets of some Afghan or Iraqi town, French farmers protesting about something or other, and David Beckham going on holiday with his new hairstyle and his family.

Hannah was interested in some of that — the hairstyle bit, particularly — but Petr only took an interest when there was a brief flurry of play from the ice hockey World Championships in Helsinki, or Stockholm or wherever. Somewhere, presumably, where they had cold winters. I wondered if it was in his bones or if Vlasta had prepared the way.

Unable to stomach yet another Sky weather forecast, I went to see how Vlasta was managing. I wasn't happy about leaving the kids alone but she had been gone ten minutes. I wasn't happy about that either. Her security awareness left a lot to be desired.

The duty-free shop was on the deck below. It was in two parts, one being the booze shop and the other the place where you got your handbags and chocolate, perfume and colour photographs of the *Pride of York*. Vlasta wasn't in either of them.

Alarm bells began to go off in my head. This wasn't good. I made a rapid reconnaissance of the obvious places. She wasn't in any of them. I began to make my way back to the kids in the upper-deck lounge.

I saw her before she saw me. She was coming through a doorway to the outer deck again. My first instinct was to call out to her. I suppressed the urge. Instead, I went outside myself. At first I thought the deck was empty. Then I saw him again — the guy with the binoculars. He was studying distant lights.

A flash of anger raced through me. She was playing games.

'So who is he?' I demanded quietly when I

got back to the table.

She looked at me with surprise.

'The bird watcher, the guy with the binoculars.'

I thought she coloured slightly with embarrassment or guilt, but I couldn't be sure. Her face was such a mess anyway.

'Vlasta?'

'I don't know what you mean.'

'Look,' I said firmly, 'if we don't trust each other, this isn't going to work. I have to know what's going on. Otherwise,' I added, 'I turn round at Zeebrugge and go home.'

'But I have paid you already!' she protested.

'I'll give you the money back.'

She thought it over but she must have known she couldn't win this one.

'All right,' she said reluctantly. 'He is a friend.'

A long-stop? Someone to keep an eye on the situation from afar? It made sense. The trouble was he wasn't very good at it. Nor was Vlasta. The guy should have been invisible, not there whenever I turned round.

'Is he English?'

She shook her head.

Boyfriend? Unlikely. But possible. I hoped that wasn't it. The situation would be more complicated than I'd thought.

'He works for Harry,' she added.

'So he might recognize anyone coming after you?'

'Yes.'

And vice-versa, of course.

'It would be better,' I said, 'to keep away from him. Let him come to you if he has anything to say.'

She nodded listlessly. I felt sorry for her. She had done, was doing, the best she could. There was a lot of responsibility on those thin shoulders. Stress, too. And she was tired.

'Come on,' I said gently. 'Let's call it a day, and get some rest.'

6

Leroy sat motionless while Harry went crazy. He had been bad enough when he discovered she had taken the kids. Now he knew she had the money as well, he was damn near berserk. Leroy didn't blame him. It was a hell of a thing. His own wife, too.

He watched as Harry kicked the wall on one side of the room and then went and did the exact same thing on the other side. Hard to tell what he would do next in this mood.

'Find her,' Harry said eventually, slowing down, thinking again. He leaned against the wall, breathing heavily. 'And if you can't find her, find the money! Do what it takes.'

'I'll find her and the money,' Leroy said, getting to his feet. He was glad to have something to do, something to get him out of here. It was no fun having to watch and listen to Harry ranting and raving.

'Maybe she won't survive?' Leroy said softly, a gleam in his eye.

'Do you think I care?' Harry retorted. 'I never want to see the bitch again.'

Leroy nodded. The way ahead seemed clear now. He liked it like that.

7

While Vlasta got the kids into bed I took a turn around our immediate vicinity. I wasn't reassured. It was a rabbit warren — vast numbers of cabins either side of extremely narrow aisles. Those on the outside had porthole windows; those in the central blocks, like ours, had no natural light whatsoever. God help us all, I thought, if anything happens to the lighting system and the ship starts sinking.

The only good thing was that no one could possibly find us in this labyrinth unless they knew the cabin number.

On second thoughts, it didn't seem so good after all. To find us, all they had to do was ask at the information desk. Any 'friend of the family' could do that without fear of refusal.

I shrugged. Nothing was going to happen tonight anyway. Probably. Harry could snatch the kids but he couldn't get them ashore. Not tonight.

As for the money in the holdall in the back of the car, well . . . For the moment I didn't even want to think about that and what it might mean.

One thing I knew: there wouldn't be much sleep for me tonight.

★ ★ ★

Vlasta opened the cabin door in response to the special knock I had told her I would use. She looked terrible but she managed a crooked smile that told me she was still coping.

'Room service!' I told her, handing over a chocolate bar I'd bought in the shop.

'And flowers?' she asked.

'Of course. They're on their way.'

She smiled. 'Chocolate is nice. Thank you, Frank.'

Her smile, even if it was a little crooked, made me feel better.

Hannah and Petr were tucked snugly up in their bunks. Each of them had a top bunk in the four-bunk set-up. That suited me; it was better for Vlasta and me to be near the ground. Not that I intended sleeping much, but I would want to sit down, perhaps even lie down.

I looked at my watch. Just gone ten. The disco and the casino would be alive for a couple of hours yet. The cinema and the bars, too. But here it was quiet, apart from the throb and vibration coming from the ship's engines, and the creak of wall panelling constantly on the move.

'Tired?' I asked.

Vlasta nodded.

'Get some sleep, then.'

'What about you?'

'I'm OK. I'll just rest a while. Read my newspaper.'

She didn't wait for a second invitation. She was under her duvet almost before I'd finished speaking.

I settled down, too. It would be a long night, with a long day to follow.

★ ★ ★

It was warm in the cabin, too warm for me, the only one left awake. I stretched out on my bunk, and by the light from the little lamp on the wall began to read my newspaper.

Times like that are not best for considering really pressing issues — like should Britain enter the Eurozone, or the constitutional reform of parliament. I spent all of five minutes on them and then I turned to the back page to see why Man U were a spent force (it wasn't a northern paper, obviously). Their players and their manager were over the hill, apparently, and the whole club was in desperate need of renewal. Nothing that Chelsea-scale invest-ment couldn't put right, though.

Then the inevitable happened and I fell asleep.

Something woke me up. I didn't know what. I lay still and tense beneath my canopy of newspaper while I worked it out.

My reading light was on still. I could see no one standing on the small area of floor between the bunks and the door. The door to the bathroom compartment was shut. Had one of the others gone in there? I could hear nothing but the steady creaking of wood and plastic, and the periodic vibration of the ship's engines.

Satisfied no intruder was in the cabin, I let the newspaper slide to the floor and sat up. I saw then that the duvet on Vlasta's bunk was thrown back. She was not there. The bathroom? I couldn't hear anything.

I stood up. Hannah was still in place, in the bunk above Vlasta's. Her head was popped out of one end of her still neatly arranged duvet. Above me, Petr looked as if he had been dreaming of battlefields. His duvet was around his ankles.

I took the two paces that got me to the bathroom door.

'Vlasta?' I whispered, lightly brushing the door with my knuckles. 'Are you in there?'

No reply. I tried the handle and the door opened, spilling light into the cabin. She wasn't there.

I closed the bathroom door gently and stood for a moment. It must have been the sound of the cabin door closing that had woken me. Damn! I should never have laid down. Where the hell was she? More to the point, had she gone voluntarily?

I opened the cabin door and glanced out into the empty corridor. Plastic doors and walls, gleaming in reflected light and creaking continually, stretched as far as I could see. Somewhere on the ship people were awake and doing their job, but here it was as quiet as a church on a Monday morning.

What to do? There wasn't much I could do for the moment. I would have to wait — and hope. My priority had to be the children.

It was entirely possible that Vlasta had just gone out for some air, in which case I hoped she was taking good care.

I walked quickly along to the next corridor intersection to see if she was there. She wasn't. I hoped to God she hadn't gone on deck. That was no place to be at night at the best of times.

I returned to the cabin, closed the door gently and sat down to wait.

It was about twenty minutes later that I heard something, the scrape of someone brushing against the external wall or door. I stood and moved to the wall adjacent to the door. I heard a key being inserted gently in the lock. With a slight squeak the door began to open.

I grasped the edge of the door with one hand and pulled hard, at the same time clamping down with the other hand on the arm of the person operating the key. There was a surprised gasp, and a body flew past me in a haze of perfume. I managed to stop myself hitting it.

I grimaced, sighed and reached down to pick Vlasta up from the floor. I gave her a hug. 'Sorry!' I whispered. 'I didn't know who it was.'

She gave a little whimper, pressed her face hard against my chest for a moment and then broke away.

'It's all right,' she said, her moment of weakness overcome. 'I didn't want to wake anyone,' she added.

'Where've you been?' I asked. 'How can I help you if you keep disappearing on me like this?'

She stood still and nodded in the half-light from the corridor. I took a look outside. The corridor remained empty. I closed the door.

'Frank, I am very worried.'

'Why? What is it?'

'My friend, Libor, the man with the binoculars. He is not there.'

'Where?'

She took a deep breath, and tried and failed to say more. I eased her down to sit on her bunk, and sat beside her. 'Take your time,' I said.

She sniffed, close to tears, and tried again.

'I was supposed to meet Libor at this time, but he was not there.'

I glanced at my watch automatically, and thought one in the morning was a hell of a time to be meeting anyone.

'He was not there,' she repeated. 'So I went to his cabin, and he was not there too.'

'Either,' I said automatically.

'Excuse me?'

'Either, not . . . It doesn't matter. He's in the bar, maybe, or at the disco?'

She shook her head. 'Everything is finished. All passengers are in their cabins, I think. Libor's door was not locked. I opened it. The light was on but he was not there. I waited, and waited, but he did not return.'

She stared at me in the semi-dark and said, 'I feel something is wrong. Libor is reliable. He would be there if he could be.'

'Something's happened to him, you mean?'

She nodded.

I mulled it over. She might be right.

'Where were you to meet him?'

'On the deck.'

'Where I saw you before?'

She nodded.

If anything had happened to him, it wasn't difficult to guess where he was now. A man like Harry, or whoever he had working for him, wouldn't have had any compunction about tipping him over the side.

'What do you think?' she asked.

'I'll check his cabin again in a little while. If he's still not there, I'll report him missing. But you'll have to be prepared, Vlasta. If he doesn't reappear, I don't think he'll be found on the ship.'

She took a moment to take that in. Then she gasped.

'Who is he?' I asked, wondering again if he was more than a friend.

'He is from my country.'

'Yes, but . . .'

'You mean do I sleep with him?'

She turned to face me and I could feel the heat from her glower. I shrugged.

'He is a friend, my only friend here. He was my interpreter when I first came to England. Harry brought him, but he came to hate Harry. So he helped me.'

'Interpreter? You needed one?'

'Until I learned some English, yes.'

'You were already married?'

She shook her head. 'I was an exotic dancer

60

— a stripper. A good one. Harry wanted me for his club.'

That stopped me in my tracks. For the moment I had no more questions.

*　*　*

Somehow we got through the night. At 6.30 I toured the ship, looking for the man with the binoculars amongst the early risers and the hungry souls heading hopefully towards the restaurant and the coffee shop. I didn't see him.

His cabin was as Vlasta had described it — unlocked. Things all over. Not particularly untidy. More like a cabin the occupant was expecting to return to imminently. An open travel bag. A sweater tossed aside. Shoes near the door. Toilet articles in the bathroom. There was nothing there that was particularly valuable or personal, but a normal person wouldn't voluntarily abandon such things without good reason. In any case, where would he go?

Vlasta studied my face anxiously when I returned. I shrugged and said I hadn't seen him. She looked devastated.

'What can have happened?' she asked.

I didn't answer. I didn't want to get into speculation along those lines. Instead, I said I would report him as missing. Vlasta said she would come with me.

I considered warning her against saying what time she had first noticed him missing, but decided against it. A meeting planned for one in the morning might raise suspicions, but so would being found out in a lie.

'Remember, Vlasta, that it was *we*, not just *you*, who looked for him last night.'

For a moment she was uncomprehending. Then she nodded and gave a rueful smile. 'You are thinking of my reputation?' she said.

'Amongst other things.'

Initially, we spoke to a woman at the information desk. She seemed to have her doubts but she called in the purser, I think it was, who took us into a cubicle of an office behind the scenes.

'Let me get this straight,' he said. 'Your friend is missing?'

'Since last night,' I told him.

'How do you know?'

'We arranged to meet him, and he didn't show up. We went to his cabin. It was unlocked but he wasn't there, and that's still the situation.'

He looked pensive for a moment.

'What time was that?'

His eyebrows went up when I told him. 'The bars were all closed by then . . . '

'I know, but we had business to discuss.'

'He was alone — a single man?'

'Yes,' Vlasta told him.

'So he might have . . . might have found company for the night?'

'Libor? Oh, no!' Vlasta said. 'He wouldn't.'

'Besides,' I added, 'our meeting was too important.'

The purser nodded and said briskly, 'Right. We'll put out a call for him to report to any ship's officer. If there's no response in ten minutes we'll search the ship.'

He shrugged apologetically and said, 'We dock at eight. So there isn't much more we can do.'

'I understand,' I told him.

We left and went to breakfast. Over coffee, Vlasta said, 'They won't find him, will they?'

I shrugged and admitted I didn't know.

'Maybe he fell overboard?' Hannah interjected, with all the callous disregard of the young.

'Into the sea?' Petr inquired.

'Of course not!' Vlasta said.

But I reckoned Hannah and Petr had it about right. Who might have helped him fall into the sea, though? That was what worried me.

8

'Your wife?'

'My wife,' Harry agreed. 'But don't worry. I've got my best man on it.'

'It's a lot of money.'

'It is. But, like I said, everything is in hand.' Harry beamed in what he intended to be a reassuring manner. 'A small delay only. Then we will be back on course.'

Harry didn't like the hand he had been dealt. Bloody Vlasta! But he couldn't fold. He had to play it as best he could.

His visitor looked a tough little bugger. He sat there silent and stone-faced. Hard to know what was going on behind that mask. The fact that he didn't know his way around this territory meant nothing. He came with strong credentials. On his own patch he was an operator. That meant something.

Harry was taking nothing for granted. There was a lot at stake. But he believed he'd done enough to allay the suspicions. He waited now for confirmation.

'The agreement still stands,' his visitor said at length. 'I leave this problem with you, Harry.'

Harry nodded and shook hands with the visitor and his companion, an equally dour man who had said nothing at all throughout the meeting. He was looking forward to seeing the back of them both.

*   *   *

Afterwards, between themselves, the visitor and his companion spoke in their own language. It was a relief to do so.

The companion said, 'You didn't tell him we would help?'

'No.'

'He will find out.'

'So? What's he going to do?'

'Probably nothing.'

'Exactly,' the visitor said. 'So let him find out. He will understand then that we are serious people, and not to be underestimated.'

9

Libor didn't show. I saw the purser again shortly before we returned to the car. He told me they would continue searching, but, with regret, they were running out of places to look.

'If he hasn't hidden himself away,' he added with a guarded look at me, 'and you give me no reason to think he might have done, then the only realistic possibility is that he fell overboard during the night.'

I just nodded.

'Had he been drinking?'

'I very much doubt it,' I told him. 'He's not that kind of guy. Besides, we saw him a few hours earlier and he was perfectly normal and sober then.'

'Then I'm sorry.' He glanced at his watch and added apologetically, 'I'm afraid this is a busy time for us.'

'Of course.'

He had maybe a thousand passengers to consider. There was no way he could hold them all up. Accidents, disappearances at sea happened. Life went on.

'If you care to present yourselves at our

office on shore, you will be looked after while the search continues.'

'Thanks.'

We shook hands and parted. I didn't tell him we couldn't wait.

Vlasta and the children were waiting outside for me. Vlasta searched my face for signs of hope, but I had none to give.

'What will happen?' she asked.

'They'll continue searching,' I said with a shrug. 'But there's nothing more we can do. We'd better just get on — if that's what you still want to do?'

'Yes. We must.' She drew herself up and I could see the determination pulsing through her. 'We will go now.'

We began to make our way down the narrow staircase to the car deck. We were in a crowd, a slow moving crowd, and I kept a sharp eye on what was happening around us. I was convinced Libor's disappearance had not been an accident, which meant Harry did have someone on board the ship.

We ourselves were now entering a particularly dangerous phase. Once we were ashore would be a good time to try to snatch the children. So as soon as we were in the car I used the central locking button to make sure no door would open unless I wanted it to. That wouldn't stop a hammer through a window but it would slow things down and give me a chance.

I was on edge. So was Vlasta. We had nothing to say to each other. And the children, in the back, were for the moment silent and forgotten.

In impatient columns vehicles poured off the ferry and we wound our way between the dockside buildings, heading for the exit. It was a wet morning in Belgium. The cloud base was low. Soft rain was sweeping in, seemingly from all directions. It was dismal and dark. Our lights were on and the wipers slapped back and forth across the windscreen. Welcome to Europe.

As we inched towards the kiosks at the unguarded exit, my eyes flicked continually between the vehicles all around us. So far, I had seen nothing to alert me. But I knew that whoever had disposed of Vlasta's friend quite possibly had us in their sights right now. We were hemmed in, and it was not a comfortable experience. I wanted to be out on the open road.

Vlasta had an EU passport, I had been relieved to note in Hull. So did each of the kids. One complication avoided. Ahead of us, people were holding up their passports and being nodded through if what they had were EU passports. One or two cars were pulled aside. But when our turn came, we, too, were nodded through.

'They don't take their work very seriously,' Vlasta commented.

'We have open borders these days.'

She seemed almost disappointed. I wasn't. I concentrated on following the cars in front of us as, still in line, we wound our way through the concrete channels that gave a speedy departure from Zeebrugge, a town of which we saw virtually nothing. Within minutes we were on a divided highway, heading, like everyone else, towards Brussels.

'This direction suit you?' I asked, beginning to relax.

'Yes, thank you.'

'Don't forget to tell me left or right when we reach the end of Belgium.'

She threw me a little smile and said, 'Now you make fun of me.'

'Me? Nah!'

But I wasn't as cheerful as I tried to appear. I had no idea where we were headed, now we were out of Zeebrugge. This was unknown territory for me. I just had to hope Vlasta knew what she was doing, and where we were going.

★ ★ ★

A wet, murky morning. Tyres hissed on watery roads. The occasional pedestrian was head-down against the driving rain. Vlasta smiled at me, a smile of relief. She seemed glad to be back on the European mainland. Understandable. All our damp little islands had given her were trouble — and two children, of course.

'Feeling better?' I asked.

She nodded.

'The swelling's going down,' I added, glancing at her face.

'Maybe.' She pulled down the vanity mirror on the passenger side and studied her face. 'Maybe,' she repeated, 'but I will never be beautiful again.'

She was serious, too.

'Come on! Your looks don't change just because you get a few bruises.'

'You should have seen me before,' she said, settling back in her seat. 'I was special then.'

'You're beautiful still,' I said to encourage her.

I didn't want a depressive on my hands. Besides, she really was a looker, still, whatever torments she had been through.

She touched my arm with her fingers in gratitude and settled back in her seat. She was tired. We both were. Missing one night's sleep is no great hardship, but for all I knew

Vlasta might have missed a few more than that. So she settled back, leaving me to smile and muse on the vanity of an ex-stripper.

Hannah and Petr were quiet, too. As the rain splattered on the roof, they burrowed ever deeper under the travel rugs in the back.

I didn't mind. I preferred few distractions while I reacquainted myself with driving on the wrong side of the road. The driving was easy, though. Just a convoy of vehicles making their way steadily through the downpour, mostly at a steady 80 kph, the local speed limit. No need to overtake. We weren't in a hurry. I just kept my distance from the car in front and made sure the one behind didn't get too close.

I felt more comfortable now. I pulled up at a red traffic light and sat waiting patiently. The rain was even heavier, pattering noisily on the roof and streaming down the windscreen and the side windows.

The vehicle in front was also a big one, a Range Rover. These four-wheel drive machines had become very popular in modern times, but I wasn't convinced they were the best thing to have for high-speed driving on good roads. Fashion accessories, more like it.

They were spacious and comfortable, though, I supposed, counting the four adult heads in the one in front. If you had a big family, or a family of big people, you needed that capability. Or if you were going on holiday with your mates, all keen outdoor enthusiasts and laden with sports gear.

I watched absently as the doors of the Range Rover opened and several figures stepped out into the rain. Fishing. Golf. That sort of holiday. Stacks of gear.

Not baseball bats, though, I suddenly realized as a couple of the figures turned our way.

Shit! My foot leaped to the throttle and I hauled desperately on the steering wheel. We took off with a roar and a screech of tyres. One of the sportsmen in front jumped out of the way and took a swing at us as we passed. The baseball bat smashed into the back of the car with a boom that made my ears ring. Someone screamed with terror. I kept going. We dropped down the embankment at the side of the road and plunged through a stream. The virtues of four-by-fours were soon evident.

It was a rough ride. The other side of the stream was a damp meadow full of black-and-white cows that watched with interest as we ripped across the hummocky grass. In the bouncing rear-view mirror I could see we were being pursued. The Range

Rover was maybe fifty yards behind. I hoped to hell we didn't stall or get stuck in soft ground.

'Did you recognize any of them?' I yelled at Vlasta, who was twisted round in her seat and staring backwards.

'No!'

I wasn't surprised. She'd probably been asleep.

'Hang on everyone!' I shouted as the embankment on the far side of the field loomed large.

We tore up the slope and smashed our way through a timber fence. I turned left on to a narrow dirt lane and sped back to rejoin the main road. There, we turned right and headed for Brussels once again. Harry's men had not gained any ground so far as I could see. Bastards! The adrenaline racing, I snarled angrily and pushed my foot down, testing the power of the machine.

I stuck to the main road, and the company of other vehicles. Hopefully, somewhere there would be a police car amongst them. Besides, the last thing I wanted was to shoot off down a country lane and find the way blocked by a farm vehicle or a megaton lorry delivering oil or cattle feed, with Harry's boys coming up fast behind us.

The Range Rover settled in a little way

behind. After that mad excursion, they were going to bide their time and take their chance when, inevitably, it came again. I grimaced at the mirror. Somehow I had to get rid of them. Somehow.

I wasn't the only one living on his nerves' edge. Vlasta had clambered into the back to attend to Petr, who was crying. Hannah was sitting upright, shocked rigid by our terrifying ride across fields. I winced. Poor kids. It was a pity they had to be involved.

'What happens after Brussels?' I asked when Vlasta regained her seat.

'Keep on going.'

'On this road? The E40?'

'Yes.'

'And then?'

'Into Germany. Aachen, and then Köln.'

'Köln? Oh, yes. Cologne.'

She nodded.

I waited. She said nothing more. I looked at her expectantly.

'Across Germany,' she added.

'All the way?'

'Yes. To the east. Dresden, perhaps.'

It was irritating to have to drag information out of her like this, but now wasn't the time to be having a debate about client trust. At least I knew now where we were headed in the next few hours, but I did wonder if

Dresden would be the end of the road.

There was one thing more I needed to know from her.

'Do they know where we're going?'

She hesitated.

'Come on, Vlasta! Does Harry know?'

She shook her head and said he didn't, but I wasn't convinced. I laboured the point. 'So if we can lose that lot behind, they won't be able to pick us up again?'

Again she said no. For the moment, I had to be satisfied with that.

⋆ ⋆ ⋆

More pressing was the need to find a way of getting out of the Range Rover's sight. Soon. Before we hit the heavy morning traffic and jams around Brussels. If they managed to get alongside us in stationary or slow moving traffic that would be it.

Forty more miles to Brussels.

'What about the money?' I said.

'The money?'

'In the bag, in the back of the car.'

She said nothing.

'Whose is it? Harry's?'

'I don't want to talk about it.'

I let it go for now. We would have to pick that one up again. I didn't know then what a million sterling looked like in big denomination notes, but my guess was that it would look very like what was in the holdall in the back of the car. So it wasn't surprising that we had four big guys with baseball bats after us. I was going to earn my meagre ten grand.

$$\star \quad \star \quad \star$$

'Have you brought a road map?' I asked, studying the rear-view mirror.

They had made no move to come up on us. Perhaps they had orders not to do anything to endanger Hannah and Petr, and were biding their time. At some point, though, we would be forced to stop or slow down. Perhaps for another red light, a road works or a traffic jam on the Brussels ring road. Or for fuel.

I was beginning to sweat. We needed to lose them but I didn't think we could out-run them. Once we were stopped, Hannah and Petr might be all right, but I wouldn't give much for Vlasta's chances — or for mine.

'What will we do?' Vlasta asked anxiously, turning to look through the rear window.

'Escape?'

Thankfully, she smiled. So she hadn't lost her nerve. She wasn't panicking. Yet. Perhaps this was nothing compared with taking your clothes off in front of a room full of goggling men. Courage comes in many forms.

'We'll have to lose them soon,' I admitted. 'They won't try anything while we're on the motorway, but if we have to stop for any reason . . . '

She nodded. She knew what I meant.

'Have you got a road map?' I asked again.

'Just this road atlas.'

'Open it on the page where we are now.'

She did. I glanced at it. 'Right,' I said, 'we're taking the Antwerp road. It's coming up.'

'But I — '

'Trust me, Vlasta!'

She shut up and let me swing onto the E17 when we reached it. I made the switch with the kind of last-minute, unsignalled manoeuvre that sensible people everywhere would scream with rage about, dodging between trucks that were nose to tail in the inside lane. The Range Rover failed to force its way through the line of trucks and missed the turn. I grunted with satisfaction. Vlasta looked at me but kept quiet.

'They'll be coming back just as soon as they reach another turn-off,' I said, 'but by then we'll be back on the road to Brussels.'

I switched lanes, circled on the clover leaf, completed the manoeuvre and got us headed again in our original direction. No sign of the

Range Rover now. Either it was way ahead or had already turned off. For the time being, at least, we'd broken free. I could start to breathe again. Maybe stop sweating.

Back on the E40, Vlasta said, 'That was clever.'

'Thank you.'

I threw her a grin. She responded.

'Now,' I suggested, 'perhaps we can settle down and cover some ground in peace.'

Belgium was a busy country that morning. Everyone was travelling to or from Brussels, mostly at high speed. The miles, the kilometres rather, ticked away. Soon we hit the Brussels ring road and the traffic congestion that might well have been the death of us if we hadn't lost the Range Rover. We worked our way round the system, shifting from one slow-moving column to another, switching lanes, watching out for filters and exits. I waited until we were out the other side and in lighter traffic heading for Liege before raising some of the questions I still wanted discussed.

'Feel like talking?'

Vlasta just looked at me.

'How come you're in this position, for a start?'

She shrugged and said, 'It is hard to explain.'

'Like to try?'

She sighed, but probably realized she had little choice now.

'My big mistake was to misunderstand Harry originally. I thought he was a good man, an English gentleman. My next mistake was to marry him. Everything followed from that.'

So far, it sounded like a conventional relationship turned bad, and headed for the divorce court. Mind you, I did wonder how even a foreign girl could mistake Harry for an English gentleman.

'Where did you meet him?'

'In Prague. I danced there in a very select club. He was there on business and saw me.'

'I thought clubs like that had rules about their girls fraternizing with their clients?'

'Yes. Usually they do. But Harry was clever. He knows how things work. So he found out where I lived and visited me there. I was surprised, but he was charming and — and so English!'

She should have seen him coming. That was my thought. No one falls for a dancer in a club any more, if they ever did outside the movies.

'He wined and dined me, and we went places. He had plenty of money. He had businesses. He wanted me to visit, and to see his club. I wasn't sure, but I did. It was very nice. I was flattered. He talked and talked. I stayed. We became married after a few months, and everything was wonderful for a time, a short time.'

'Until?'

She was silent for a long time, thinking it over.

'I don't know,' she said, 'but things changed. He wanted me to contact girls I knew at home, and to bring them to his club. At first, he wanted them to dance, and then . . . And then do other things, as well.'

'Prostitution?'

She nodded.

'Then he wanted me to dance sometimes. Sometimes I did, but I didn't like it. Not now we were married. It wasn't the same.

'I think,' she said, looking at me defiantly, 'he became bored with me, as with all his other girls. I refused to dance any more. He got angry. Then things fell apart.

'Maybe he really did want me to begin with, but that was before I knew what a violent man he was. And before I knew about some of his businesses. They are not all legal,' she added unnecessarily.

The effort of trying to explain things had drained her. Now she fell silent. I left her to it. Her tale was sad but far from unusual. The big difference was that Harry was a pretty special kind of guy. You don't walk away from someone like Harry intact — if you ever walk away at all — and certainly not if you're taking his kids and a big bag full of his money.

10

A couple of hours later we had left Brussels and then Liege behind, were out of Belgium and were approaching Cologne. The rain had stopped and occasionally a streak of sunshine made a fleeting appearance. To round things off, the kids were slumbering quietly, Vlasta was pensive and I still didn't know what the hell was happening. Somehow I had to bring the drip-feeding of information to an end and get Vlasta to give me the full story. She didn't have to trust me; she just had to help me help her. Otherwise, I still had the option of bailing out.

After negotiating the lane switches that took us around the edge of Cologne, we made a brief stop at a service station and went inside the coffee shop. The kids were hungry, I needed coffee and Vlasta wanted to look at her face in a decent mirror and attempt some more repairs. I bought a tray of breakfast stuff and then Vlasta departed for the Ladies.

Hannah was feeling grown-up and responsible. She rebuked Petr for making a mess on the table with his frankfurter. It fell out, he protested. She snapped at him then in that language they sometimes used together. It subdued him. He abandoned the partially chewed sausage and turned to his fruit juice.

'What language was that?' I asked Hannah.

'Czech, of course.'

Of course. Czech. Why didn't I think of that?

'Is that where we're going — where the Czechs live?'

Hannah guffawed. 'Yes, silly! We're going to visit Grandmother and Grandfather. We will stay with them.'

Entirely reasonable. And a bad mistake. Harry George wouldn't be up to much if he hadn't thought of that.

'Looking good!' I told Vlasta when she returned.

She wasn't, but she gave me a wan smile. Maybe the swelling had gone down a bit, though. And her make-up concealed some of the bruising.

We were on the road again a couple of minutes later. The traffic was quieter east of Cologne, and the driving more relaxed. We sped along at a steady 70 mph, just below the German speed limit. In other circumstances I would have switched on the cruise control and sat back. Not now, though. I couldn't afford to be that relaxed.

So we were going where the Czechs lived,

the Czech Republic. Most of them, at least. There were probably still plenty in Slovakia, the other half of what used to be Czechoslovakia. No thanks to Vlasta, I now had a better idea of our destination.

But why Dresden first? If we went that far east in Germany, we would be in danger of bypassing the Czech Republic altogether and running into Poland. I'd have to wait until we had another service stop and see if I could squeeze some more information out of Hannah.

Still on the E40, we were sweeping past Siegen when it happened. There were rest places every few miles, where you could pull off the autobahn and stretch your legs or get your head down for a while. As we neared one, a Range Rover appeared in my rear-view mirror, part of a speeding column of Mercedes and BMWs in the fast lane. My eyes stuck to it.

Then it all happened so fast. I was mentally prepared to take evasive action but I was caught, boxed in by a slow-moving wagon in front and cars behind. The Range Rover drew alongside and moved across my front, trying to force me off the road. We made heavy contact.

My options were limited. I swung onto the shoulder and into the rest place at high speed, ploughing through a line of road signs, the Range Rover virtually fastened to the front corner of our vehicle.

Vlasta screamed. Tearing metal screeched. We scattered a bunch of waste bins, narrowly missed a line of heavy, timber picnic tables and flattened a couple of young trees. We were slowing but I didn't want to stop. I wanted to drive through the rest place and out the other end.

The Range Rover continued pressing us sideways. The back of a huge parked wagon loomed. I jerked desperately at the steering wheel and somehow we broke away from the Range Rover. I kept the steering wheel locked down. We veered to the left of the lorry, our back-end glancing it a blow.

I changed down and kept my foot hard to the floor and we raced the length of the wagon, people scattering out of our way. We cleared the front of the wagon. I glimpsed the Range Rover behind us on the other side. They'd lost ground. I kept going, speeding between the lines of parked vehicles. I overtook a car moving fast towards the exit, ignoring the frantic gesticulations from the driver.

In the wing mirror I caught a brief view of the Range Rover as it hit a high kerb and somersaulted, end over end. Doors and other components rapidly detached themselves from the main body and flew through the air like a flock of ungainly birds.

We reached the access lane back on to the autobahn and headed out at max speed, slipping between a couple of big lorries and then dodging through lines of traffic in the two outer lanes.

There was no Range Rover behind us now, and I knew there wouldn't be again.

★   ★   ★

Twenty minutes later I pulled off the road into another rest place. Leaving the engine running, I threw open the door and climbed out to assess the damage.

The side was gouged the full length of the vehicle. The front corner on the driver's side was crunched, the lights smashed. The back end was badly dented. But there was no steam jetting out from beneath the bonnet, and all the tyres were intact.

I jumped back in and got us moving again. A glance at the dials suggested most things were working. Our damage was superficial. Bodywork only. It wasn't going to stop us.

My passengers were silent. Still stunned, I assumed. I said nothing. I had no time or energy for conversation. We needed to put some distance between ourselves and what had happened.

Another twenty minutes and then I pulled into a big service area. I headed round past the petrol pumps and the shop, on past the tourist buses and the holiday makers. I headed for the far side of the parking area and stopped behind a line of wagons.

I sat for a few moments, eyes closed, hands gripping the steering wheel hard. Then I switched off the engine and turned to Vlasta.

'You OK?'

She nodded.

I turned and checked that the kids were all right, scared but unhurt.

'Right, Vlasta. What's going on?'

'I have told you already,' she said, stony faced.

'No.' I shook my head and gave a bitter little laugh. 'I didn't bargain for anything like this. We could all have been killed back there. Deliberately. By your husband.'

'No, not Harry!'

'What? You think it was someone else, or an accident?'

She shrugged.

'As it is,' I added brutally, 'we may have killed those maniacs in the Range Rover.'

She stared hard through the windscreen for a moment. Then she unbuckled her seat belt, got up and turned to the children. She spoke to them. Petr was crying now. Hannah was under the travel rug. Probably terrified, and rigid with fear.

'If you won't tell me where we're going,' I said angrily, 'then tell me how the hell Harry knows!'

She said nothing. Nothing. She wasn't giving an inch. Not a word of explanation, still less apology or information.

'OK,' I said. 'You're on your own.'

I got out of the car, walked round the back, opened the rear door and took out my bag. I pulled the door down and slammed it shut. Then I set off walking towards the building where people paid for their petrol.

It was a couple of hundred yards away and I figured by the time I got there I should have calmed down enough to be capable of phoning for a hire car to get me out of there. Vlasta could figure out for herself what she was going to do. I thought about returning her money. Then I thought, the hell with it. I'd earned it already. And she had enough money in the back of the car to hire an army of bodyguards and flunkeys. Let her do it.

I could have felt desperately sorry for the kids but I blotted them out. They weren't mine, and they weren't my responsibility either. There was nothing I could do for them.

'Frank!'

I kept on walking.

'Frank, wait!'

I didn't look round.

Running feet sounded behind me.

She grabbed my arm. 'Wait, please!'

I stopped reluctantly and turned to face her.

'You did well back there,' she said. 'Really well. I know it. I am in shock. I didn't expect this any more than you did. This isn't Harry.'

I stared at her. Her face had lost that sullen, blank look. She looked close to tears now. I knew it could be an act but I began to relent.

'So if it wasn't Harry, who was it?'

She shook her head. I couldn't tell if that meant she didn't know or she wasn't going to tell me.

'OK. Try this one. Where are we going, Vlasta? After Dresden?'

Even then she hesitated. But she looked into my eyes and saw what was there: I had limits. She knew it. And she knew I was close to them.

'OK. I will tell you. But first I must make phone call.'

I was still tempted. There was nothing to

stop me continuing on to the coffee shop and calling for a hire car. An hour, and I could be at an airport. Bonn or Frankfurt. Take my pick. Be home again in time for tea.

I could leave this vulnerable, troubled, threatened woman and her two children to their own devices. By tonight I could be reminiscing with Jimmy Mack again about times when the sea boiled with fish.

Oh, shit!

'Make your phone call, Vlasta.' I turned and set off back to the car. 'Make it quick.'

11

'Sorry about all the bumps and bangs, kids,' I said as I got back into the car. 'It's a really rough road.'

'Rough road?' Hannah said, her disbelief threatening to become outrage. 'Frank!'

'What?'

'You bumped into them!' Petr cried. 'You're a terrible driver, absolute rubbish.'

'Me?'

I heard Hannah giggle. Then Petr chortled. I smiled with relief. They were recovering.

'I'm going to drive over to that shop,' I said, 'just as soon as your mum gets back. I'm going to see if they have ice cream.'

'They should do,' Hannah said, clambering upright so she could peer through the windscreen.

'You think?'

Petr climbed up, too. 'They might have ice cream,' he announced, having given it a lot of consideration.

'That's what I think,' I said.

I watched Vlasta walking quickly back to the car. Something about her posture concerned me. She was sort of huddled, worried. She had a lot on her mind, of course. I just hoped there wasn't something extra to worry about.

She got in. She stared through the windscreen. She said nothing.

I started up and drove over to the shop. I parked close to the entrance. She looked at me.

'Ice cream,' I said.

She was uncomprehending.

'I promised the kids.'

She nodded and went back to staring through the windscreen.

★ ★ ★

'So?' I said, ice creams duly distributed.

'I have bad news,' Vlasta said.

'Oh?' I somehow refrained from adding that that made a change.

'I said I would tell you where we would go.'

'You did, yes.'

'We were going to Dêĉín, in Northern Bohemia.'

'Near Dresden?'

'Fifty or sixty kilometres away, in the Czech Republic. My parents live there.'

I knew that already.

'So?'

'We can't go there now. My mother said

Harry has phoned them. He is on his way there.'

That wasn't a surprise. What else could you expect? Even if Harry didn't want Vlasta back, he would want the kids and the money. And going home to Mother was a pretty predictable thing for a disenchanted wife to do. I was almost disappointed with Vlasta.

'So what do you want to do?'

'We will go to Šumava,' she announced briskly. 'My family used to have holidays there. I know the area well.'

'Does Harry know it, as well?'

She shook her head.

'OK.'

I started the engine. We would go to Šumava, wherever that was. Maybe we would think of something else along the way. And maybe Vlasta's parents would be OK entertaining Harry. It wasn't my job to doubt it. I had enough on my plate.

The kids were one thing. But it was the money that really worried me, all those bank notes. Bad things tend to happen when money like that is lying around.

★ ★ ★

Something else still worried me, as well. The ease with which we had been intercepted

93

more than once suggested Harry's men had not been working blind. Then there was the ferocity of the attacks. I wondered if Harry knew how reckless his men were, or if Vlasta was right in suggesting it wasn't his doing.

After another few miles I pulled over again into a rest place and ran another quick check on the car. This time I was looking for a tracker device. I was sure there was one. But it could be anywhere. Nothing under the edges of the car, or the bumpers. I got down full-length on the ground but could see nothing underneath that shouldn't be there. It could be anywhere, even in the petrol tank. I gave up.

'What is it?' Vlasta asked.

I grimaced as I got back up. 'I think we're sending out a homing signal. We must be. But I can't find the bug. I would have to take the car to pieces, or use a detector.'

I looked at her and added, 'We should change cars. Drop this one.'

She shook her head. 'No.'

'No?'

'We can't.'

'There's enough money in the bag, there, to buy a hundred cars.'

But I could see she wasn't going to budge.

'OK,' I said with a sigh. 'But we can expect your friends to appear again — unless they were all killed back there.'

She had returned to silent mode. Deep in thought. Struggling with what I had told her.

'You suggested it might not have been Harry who was responsible for the attacks,' I reminded her. 'So who could it have been?'

She shrugged.

I stared at her.

'I don't know,' she said. 'Maybe it was. Maybe I made a mistake. I have told you everything,' she added, as I continued to stare at her. 'Everything I know.'

Oh, yeah! Sure she had.

Now I trusted Vlasta about as much as she trusted me. For all I knew, Harry George could be a really wonderful guy, a perfect husband and father, and she'd told me a pack of lies.

Oh, yeah!

★   ★   ★

We drifted the rest of that first day. We left the E40 and eased our way down to Bamberg and Nuremburg. Then we headed east, into the hills and up towards the Czech border. The travelling was slow, the road no longer high-speed autobahn. We were caught in lines of lorries straining up the inclines and through the forests. I didn't mind moving more steadily. There had been enough excitement for one day.

That night we spent in a small motel near Odrava, just inside the Czech Republic. We were all tired, exhausted even. We ate in the restaurant downstairs, and then Vlasta and the kids retired to our room. I went outside to check the car and to think things through for a few minutes in the cool, clear air.

It was only a little place, a hamlet with a scattering of buildings, mostly commercial. A couple of garages. A few guest houses. One or two cheap restaurants, all of them 'Non-Stop', the local euphemism seemingly for twenty-four-hour opening.

There was also a brothel. I watched as the neon lights on the roof brightened and sparkled with the approach of darkness. Silhouetted figures of nubile young women cavorted on the roof of the building, repeatedly shedding their clothes and jiving to the sound of amplified music from some-where within. A couple of BMWs with German plates drew up outside, bringing early customers. Young men in business suits headed for the illuminated doorway.

It served as a reality check. I thought about Harry George and his clubs back home. I thought about Harry George and Vlasta. I knew I shouldn't forget that this was their background. Both of them. Vlasta was a mother with two nice children now, but this was where she had come from. Why had I ever thought of her as squeaky clean? What kind of woman — what kind of ex-stripper — ran from home and husband with probably a million sterling that wasn't hers in the back of her car?

What had I got myself into this time? Questions, questions. Where are you, Jimmy Mack, when I need your wise counsel?

12

Leroy pushed his way through the screaming, bleeding bodies and crawled out of the wreckage. He didn't need to open a door or a window; on his side there were none there. One of the injured men clung to his leg and begged for help. Leroy stamped on his face and shook him off. Then he stood up and made his way up a small grassed mound.

From his vantage point, Leroy watched as people ran to the stricken vehicle and attempted to pull bodies clear. The flames drove them back. One lorry driver arrived with a small fire extinguisher and started spraying foam onto the Range Rover. It wasn't enough. The flames overcame the foam. Then the fuel tank exploded.

By then, Leroy had already pulled back further from the scene. He sat at a picnic table and inspected himself. He wiped glass and grass from his face and studied his legs and arms. His clothes were a mess but he himself seemed to be all right. A few scratches and bruises only. The back of the vehicle had been a good place to sit. From there he had been able to give instructions without risking diving through the wind-screen if anything went wrong.

And it had gone wrong. Very wrong. No one else had got out of the vehicle. Not one of them. Harry wouldn't mind. They hadn't been his men. They were all useless anyway. Fucking foreigners, Leroy thought with weary disgust. Some driver they'd come up with.

He got to his feet again and began to make his way towards the toilet block in the middle of the rest area. He needed to clean himself up, get new clothes and a new car and then get out of here fast, preferably before the cops, who would undoubtedly arrive soon, had got a handle on what had happened. He also needed to make a couple of phone calls, one to Harry, but that could wait.

In the toilet block he washed his face and hands. He smoothed back his short hair and straightened his clothes. Then he went back outside, sat down on a bench and waited.

★   ★   ★

He didn't have long to wait. The smoke from the burning vehicle attracted even more visitors than would normally have stopped at the rest place. By the time he could hear approaching sirens he had already spotted what he wanted.

The driver of the big, black BMW was average size, just like Leroy. When he got out of the car he first paused and turned to look at the column of smoke and the attendant crowd a couple of hundred yards away. Then he made his way into the toilet block.

Leroy followed moments later. His man was using the facilities. Two others had dried their hands and were about to leave. Leroy let them go and waited until his man was washing his hands. Then he moved up quickly, wrapped one hand round the man's face and pulled back. At the same time he slid his knife in low down and held on until the brief struggle stopped.

He dragged the body into a cubicle and locked the door. He pulled off trousers and jacket, and used them to replace his own.

The car key was in a jacket pocket. Leroy nodded with satisfaction. He had everything he needed.

When he was sure no one else was in the toilet block, Leroy propped the body on the toilet seat, opened the door of the cubicle and left. It was not possible to climb out of the cubicle or to lock it. So the body would probably be discovered within minutes, but by then Leroy knew he would be well away.

He took his own clothes with him. They would be dumped elsewhere, somewhere

where there was no chance of them being linked to what had happened here.

The BMW started as he had expected it would, with great power and promise. Leroy smiled and eased his way back on to the autobahn. It had gone well. The crash had been unfortunate, as had the fact that Harry's old lady had escaped, but after that his own response had been as good as he could have wished.

★   ★   ★

An hour later, he stopped to phone Harry. He reported what had happened.

'They got away?' Harry said.

'They were lucky.'

'So she's still got the money?'

Leroy sighed. 'As far as I know, Harry. I haven't actually seen it.'

'She's got it. The guys in your car . . . I didn't know about them?'

'They were there to help.'

'Still . . . '

'There wasn't time, Harry. Things just happened. They insisted on being involved.'

'Right.'

Harry was making a big effort, Leroy thought with a smile. He was just glad he was a thousand miles away.

'But they didn't make it anyway? Just you?'

'Just me.'

'Someone's not going to be pleased.'

'Shit happens,' Leroy said with a shrug.

'You're telling me! Right. I'm going out there now. Flying. Join me as soon as you can.'

The phone went dead. Leroy scowled. Not a word of thanks. Not a 'how-are-you, Leroy?'

Then he smiled ruefully. All his life he had had to look after himself. Why did he think that would ever change?

The BMW lifted to just over the speed limit, like everyone else. He liked this car, really liked it, but he was going to have to dump it before he joined Harry. He probably had a couple of hours till the cops knew what they were looking for. No more than that, though. It was enough.

13

'How much is in the bag?' I asked her.

'Excuse me?'

'The bag in the back of the car. How much money is in it?'

She turned sideways to stare out of the window. I sped up to overtake an old lorry. We were on a blind bend but the entire road was just a series of blind bends. We couldn't trail along at 20 mph for ever.

'Perhaps a million. Maybe more.'

'Sterling?'

She nodded.

I said nothing for a moment, while I digested the idea. Perhaps a million pounds? Maybe more? Jesus Christ! I wished I hadn't asked. I'd felt better when I didn't really know, when I was just guessing.

'Vlasta, what the hell are you doing with it? Who's is it?'

As if I didn't know.

'It is mine,' she said, turning angrily on me. 'What? You think I didn't pay you enough?'

I laughed, but I wasn't amused. 'What you paid me won't do much more than pay for my funeral.'

'I will pay you more.'

'Don't bother! Just tell me where you got the bag. I need to know who's coming after us.'

'It is Harry's bag,' she said.

'And Harry's money?'

She hesitated just enough to warn me I wasn't going to get the truth.

'Yes,' she said. 'It was Harry's money.'

'And now it's yours?'

'Yes,' she said, glaring at me defiantly. 'Now it is mine. I have earned it.'

Well, there you go. First it was Harry's; now it's Vlasta's. What could be simpler?

'So who's coming after us? Harry?'

She didn't bother answering that. And I didn't bother repeating the question.

★ ★ ★

Early morning. On the road. Surprisingly, we all seemed to have had a good night's sleep. Exhaustion, physical and nervous, probably had had something to do with it. Now we were cruising through leafy lanes in South Bohemia. Initially, we were headed for Plzeň, home of such good beer. I wasn't sure after that. Šumava, Vlasta had said, but I was leaving the navigation to her. This was her home turf, and her game plan.

It was quiet country. Vast fields, empty villages, few livestock out in the open. Not much on the road. Quite a change, and a welcome one, from yesterday on Germany's speed tracks. I could have been content and relaxed. It was just the questions surrounding the bag in the back of the car that were keeping me on edge.

I tried again.

'The money . . . ' I began.

'Harry owes me. He owes the other girls he brought from my country, too. The money will help us all recover our lives.'

'It's a lot of money, though. Where's it from? His clubs?'

'The clubs are big money earners. Drugs, girls, music . . . It is good business.'

Yes, but that good?

'A million sterling, Vlasta,' I said quietly.

She frowned and squirmed, pouted and shook her head indignantly.

'Cash,' I added. 'He doesn't have a bank account? He's just been pushing it all under the bed for . . . what? Several years?'

'It is a payment,' she said sullenly.

'A payment?'

'He was going to pay somebody. At the end of the year he must make this payment. Now is the time,' she added with a shrug.

'So if he can't come up with another

million quid, he'll miss making the payment?'

She didn't answer. She didn't need to. If Harry missed the payment — it didn't matter who it was to — there would be consequences. Vlasta knew that. She was playing hardball.

And I had an idea now why she thought it might not have been Harry pursuing us with such lethal intent.

★ ★ ★

Šumava is a pretty wild area, a kind of national park that Czechs value for its wildlife, and for its cycle tracks and footpaths through the low, forested hills. It didn't always have that status, though, Vlasta told me. During the Cold War years, and perhaps earlier too, it was a fortified border region, a no-go area for civilians. That was what had made it such a haven for wildlife. When the barbed wire came down and the mines were lifted, Czechs were amazed and delighted at what they found along their border with Bavaria.

In other circumstances, so would I have been delighted with the area. The hills and forests of South Bohemia, beautiful, peaceful country now. But all I could think about was how likely was it that the owner of that bag in

106

the back of the car was going to let us enjoy the journey? How long before the next attempt to get it back?

We drove into the small village of Srni in mid-afternoon. It was dusty and hot. One of those days that suggested we were well into summer, with winter a long way behind us. Except that it had snowed the night before. There was still a thin coating on the hills.

The guest house we booked into was a pleasant, modern timber building. In winter it would be a ski lodge. Now it was a good base for walkers and cyclists. We were given a big room with several beds and an adjacent bathroom. Meals were served downstairs in a pleasant restaurant with gingham table-cloths and vases of dried flowers on the pine tables.

'I will phone my mother,' Vlasta announced.

She took her mobile outside, looking for better reception, or perhaps because she didn't want me or the kids to overhear. I was left in our room with Hannah and Petr, who were both eager to explore our new residence.

'I like it here,' Hannah announced. 'Will we stay long, Frank?'

'All night, probably,' I said with a smile.

★ ★ ★

Vlasta returned looking deathly grey. She stared at me for a moment and then flung herself onto a bed, burying her face in the pillow.

'Hannah,' I said quickly, 'can you see if that slot machine downstairs in the lobby sells chocolate bars?'

She jumped up. I gave her a handful of euros. 'See if they will change these for Czech koruna. Petr, you go as well.'

They couldn't get through the door fast enough.

'OK,' I said. 'What's the problem?'

Vlasta didn't respond.

I sat beside her and touched her arm lightly. 'Vlasta?'

She sat up and looked at me. 'It is over,' she said. 'My dream. Everything was for nothing.'

'Tell me.'

'Harry is there, in Děčín. He has my parents hostage. He said he wants the children and the money.'

I grimaced. But her news wasn't a surprise to me. 'Go on,' I said.

'There is no choice. He said I must do what he says. Otherwise I will be an orphan.'

'And you believe him?'

'Oh, yes. He means what he says. He has Leroy with him.'

That clinched it for me. I didn't know about Harry George, but I had seen enough of Leroy to be able to guess what he was capable of.

I could understand Harry's determination to reclaim the money, but were the children so important to him? Maybe it was a matter of pride or honour, or something like that. I couldn't see that looking after two children was going to fit very well with his lifestyle.

Right now, though, the priority was saving Vlasta's parents, and Vlasta's sanity.

'It is over,' she repeated bitterly.

'No,' I told her. 'No, it isn't.'

But there was no gleam of hope in her eyes when she looked at me.

14

When I phoned Bill Peart he was annoyed. It was his day off. I wasn't impressed.

'So it's all right for you to call me when I'm having a rest day, but not the other way round. Is that how it is?'

'You? Frank, you have every day off. What do you know about my working life?'

'Very busy, I'm sure. So what are you doing now?'

'Reading the paper. Reading the sports pages. The 'Boro look like starting off next season as badly as they finished last season.'

'That's a shame. About Harry George?'

'I thought you weren't going to take the job?'

'I didn't. I'm working for his wife.'

There was a long pause. Then he laughed. 'Oh, boy!'

'What?'

'You sure know how to pick your clients.'

'She's all right.'

'Sure she is — but will you be?'

'What do you mean by that?'

'Does Harry know you're working for his wife?'

'He does now.'

'Oh, boy!'

I was getting tired of his attitude.

'Harry's business,' I said. 'Is it going well?'

'Which one?'

'Hell, I don't know! All of them.'

'Well, we don't think so. He's struggling, like everyone else. It doesn't matter whether the business is legitimate or not, if the punters don't have the money. And closing the steelworks at Redcar was just about the last straw.

'But we think there's a lot of money going through the books anyway, more than the business itself can generate. We also believe some serious people may have moved in with him. He might even have had an offer he couldn't refuse. If he does refuse, he loses his business anyway and we find him in the river. A sad loss to the community, not to mention humanity. That answer your question?'

It did. It also suggested a whole new way of looking at things, especially the attacks on us.

'So whose money is he laundering?'

'That's a good question.'

In other words, they didn't know.

'What are you doing for his wife, Frank?'

'Taking her home, her and the kids.'

'You're what!' There was a stunned silence.

Then he said, 'Take care, son. Where the hell are you anyway?'

'The Czech Republic. It used to be part of Czechoslovakia.'

'I know what it used to be. I've been to Prague for a boozy weekend. That where you are?'

'Not yet. Anyway, we've hit a problem.'

'That's a surprise. So you call me?'

'If Harry is laundering money,' I said, pressing on and ignoring the little provocations, 'he must have partners. Do you know who they are?'

'Not yet. But we suspect they're East European, probably Russian. The Russians have a good hold on Cyprus, where his family comes from. We think that's the link.

'I'm not sure we would call them partners, though. Maybe they are. I don't know. But if the business is underperforming, they could be big and serious enough to gobble Harry up. They're not going to let it go to the wall. They need it.'

My new perspective was growing sharper by the minute. It sounded like Harry was struggling on the business front as well as the home front.

'So what are you doing out there, Frank?'

'Harry and his boys have been playing rough. Or maybe it was someone else. A business partner, perhaps. But right now, we're having a rest.'

'You and Mrs George, and the kids, eh?'

'That's right.'

I was reluctant to tell him too much. I didn't want to make an official complaint either. I didn't want European police forces involved at this stage. My feeling was that if we went down that road, Vlasta wouldn't come out of it too well. After all, she had a big bag of money that wasn't hers, money that almost certainly had come from illegal operations. Plus she was married to an international crook who had business dealings with other international crooks. It could take a long time to sort that lot out. By then, Vlasta's parents could be dead and her kids grown up.

'Has Harry made threats, Frank?'

'You could say that. I don't want to spell them out at this stage, but you would do me a big favour if you could run past Risky Point now and then to see if my house is still there. See if Jimmy Mack is still alive, as well.'

'I can do that. What are you going to do for me?'

'I want Harry off the board, Bill. So does Vlasta. I'll help you take him down. Just give me a little time.'

Bill seemed to find that acceptable. At

least, he didn't object.

What he did say was, 'Vlasta? That's Mrs George?'

'It is.'

'You mentioned her kids?'

'Yeah. They're here with us.'

'You know they're not Harry's?'

That shut me up.

'Frank?'

'No, I didn't know that. You sure?'

'She brought them with her, from wherever the hell she came from. I don't remember now.'

I had trouble processing that bit of information. I didn't know what the hell to do with it.

'She didn't tell you?' Bill said.

'No.'

'I wonder why,' he said quietly.

So did I.

★　★　★

I stayed outside for a few minutes after I'd finished the call to Bill. It was quiet there. The conifers that came up close to the building were sighing gently in a light breeze. The sky was a bright patchwork of blue with vivid white clouds. Nice.

A small car drove along the street. A

Škoda, naturally. A couple of middle-aged men stood talking outside a bakery shop. A dog cocked its leg against a flower tub full of red geraniums.

Ordinary life. I sighed and turned to look up at our window. Hannah was there, gazing down at me. She waved. I waved back. Then I made up my mind and went back inside. They were still Vlasta's kids, even if they weren't Harry's. And I still liked them as much as ever, and wanted to protect them.

⋆   ⋆   ⋆

I took Vlasta aside.

'What?' she said.

'Compromise. We give Harry the money, but not the kids.'

She just stared at me. I got the feeling events had overtaken her. She was in way over her head now and couldn't think straight any more.

'We do that,' I said, 'and we protect your parents.'

She shuddered. 'Maybe that isn't enough.'

'It's better than giving him everything.'

I ignored her point that it might not be enough. At that stage, I was thinking we would give him the money, get rid of it, and then Vlasta could always seek protection from

Czech law and order. They ought to be more interested in Harry and the money than in her and her children.

'I'll do the handover,' I said. 'Not you. That wouldn't be safe.'

'But you wouldn't be safe.'

'I have insurance, a cop friend back home. Harry can't touch me.'

He could, of course. It might make things more difficult for him back home, but maybe that would be the least of his worries. Sorting things out right here would be top of his agenda. I hoped so anyway.

'Besides,' I told Vlasta, 'if I'm the one who gives Harry his money back, I ought to be his friend for life.'

Vlasta didn't seem to find that funny. Neither did I, actually.

'Let's go,' I said gently. 'First thing tomorrow.'

★ ★ ★

With one or two short stops, it took us about four hours to get there. On the way, I worked out the best way to handle it. I would park Vlasta and the kids somewhere safe, and then go on to the meet alone — and hope I came back again.

First, though, we swapped cars. No point

pretending we would be safe anywhere so long as we had a vehicle that was radioactive. Harry could be following our progress on a big screen or a wall map for all I knew. Sticking pins in to mark our progress.

In Plzeň we bought a new car, an Octavia, from a dealer, using some of Harry's money. The money from the bag, at least. What the dealer thought when we paid cash, I had no idea. Vlasta did the business. Maybe cash deals were still normal in that part of the world. Certainly they would be popular. They are everywhere. At any rate, he made no fuss.

We didn't even think of trading in. We just transferred our stuff to the new car and left the Land Cruiser in a Tesco car park. With considerable relief on my part, I might add. Then we moved on.

Dêčín was a pretty little town of fifty thousand people, surrounded by forested hills. It nestled in a bowl alongside a big river, the Labe, better known to me and the Germans as the Elbe. It was only five or ten miles from the German border, and about thirty from Dresden. Now I understood Vlasta's original route plan. It would have been a straightforward way to go, if only Harry hadn't been so determined on getting the money and the kids back.

Vlasta took me on a drive past her parents'

home on the outskirts. It was an area of picturesque timber houses, each detached and quite big, and each standing in large gardens full of tall trees. Quiet, secluded, empty seeming. From my point of view not at all ideal. It was a great pity they didn't live in one of the blocks of flats in the town centre.

Then we drove out of town and headed along forested roads for a few miles. We stopped in a village with an unpronounceable name: Jetřichovice. The guest house Vlasta had chosen was an old mill, apparently. Deep in the forest, it seemed ideal. She vaguely knew the place, and the owners. So long as Harry George didn't, I decided, they should all be fine there.

I waited until they were settled. Then I had Vlasta call her parents to tell Harry I was on my way. He wanted to argue, apparently, but Vlasta did what I'd said. She switched off and dropped the phone.

She looked at me with anxious, troubled eyes. I nodded. We had said all there was to say. Time now for me to go and do the business.

15

It was a thirty minute drive back into Dêĉín from Jetřichovice. I took it slowly, cruising through small villages and leafy forest along the sun-dappled road. Idyllic countryside. Soft and warm. Traditional. Stable. A sense of life having gone on here the same way for time eternity. I could have been content, happy even, to be here. Except I had Harry George to meet, and to try to survive.

It wasn't only him either. Or even him plus Leroy Whatever-his-name-was. It was the two of them plus their mysterious, dangerous business partners. I wondered who they were, the latter, and what their involvement was. Bill Peart had given me some idea, but I had nothing concrete or precise.

I didn't fully understand the current situation either. The million pounds in the bag was part of it. I could see why Harry George and, or, his business partners, wanted their money back. That was plain and simple enough. But what about the kids? I had thought Harry probably wanted them back, too, but what if they were not his?

Besides, the potentially lethal way we had

been ambushed suggested that whoever was mounting the attacks didn't give a toss whether Vlasta and the kids survived. Was that Harry going overboard, or someone else, as Vlasta had suggested?

★ ★ ★

Early evening. Traffic was light as I eased into town. People were back home in their cottages and flats, back with their families and dogs, sitting in their gardens, drinking good Bohemian pilsener beer and Moravian wine. Enjoying the good life, the life that suits most of us admirably. Not the Harry Georges, though. Nor the Leroys and the gangs on the make either. Time to be careful.

I drove past the house at a normal speed, neither fast nor slow. A couple of cars were parked there but I saw nobody in or around them. A little way along the road I pulled into the kerb and paused for a few moments, making sure I was ready. I was, I decided. As ready as I was ever going to be. I U-turned and drove back.

I parked and approached the front door of the house. Nobody appeared to stop or detain me. I pushed a button and listened to chimes playing inside the house. I heard hard heels clattering across a wooden floor.

The door opened.

A man I had not seen before stood back and motioned me in. I stepped forward into a hall that you could say was discreetly lit. A hand on my shoulder gently propelled me towards an open door.

Harry was waiting for me. He was sitting on a sofa, facing two elderly people on another sofa. Two other men were in the room, one of them being Leroy. I took all that in at a glance and focused on Harry.

He was looking debonair, as on the previous occasion we had met. A smart suit in navy, and another immaculate white shirt. No smile this time, though. He didn't need one. He didn't need to sell me anything. He wasn't buying either. He was taking.

'I warned you to keep out of it,' he said, straight to the point.

I shrugged. 'I like a good fight. And Vlasta needed some help.'

'I told you what my wife was like. Now do you believe me? She's trouble. Where is she, anyway?'

'Far from here. But I've brought your money.'

'Where is it?'

'In the car. The car's open.'

He nodded to someone behind me. I heard the door open but I didn't look round.

'Hello,' I said to the old couple on the sofa. They looked bewildered, and frightened. But the man nodded and replied in Czech.

'So where are they?' Harry asked.

I shook my head. 'You've got your money back. You can leave now, Harry. Leave them alone — these people, as well.'

I knew it was a forlorn hope, but I had to try.

'Where's my wife — and the kids?'

'A couple of hundred miles from here. Do you know Šumava?'

He just stared at me.

'That's where they are.'

He asked one of the men to question the old folk about Šumava. The answer satisfied him up to a point.

'The deal was to bring them here.'

I looked at him and shook my head. 'That was never going to happen. You've got your money back. Now go. Leave them alone.'

Harry studied me for a moment, and then said, 'You seem to think you're going to come out of it alive.'

'I'm fireproof, Harry. Anything happens to me, my friends in the Cleveland Constabulary know exactly who to go after. They know where I am right now, as well.'

'So what are they going to do?' Leroy sneered, coming into the conversation for the first time. 'They can catch bullets?'

I ignored Leroy. 'Anything happens to me, Harry, and your businesses are closed down. Your properties are sequestered. Your bank accounts frozen. Your activities publicized, Interpol alerted and an international arrest warrant issued. The Czech police brought on board. How am I doing?'

Harry shook his head. 'It's a bluff.'

'What? You think I would expose myself like this if I didn't have cover? I'll speed dial Middlesbrough CID, if you like, and let you talk to my contact there. How's that?'

He wasn't sure. Some of it was possible. He knew that. Some of it would stall in the courts. But the exposure and attention would kill him business-wise. Besides, he had things going on here and at home that I didn't understand, things that seemed to weigh heavily with him.

I felt and heard the door behind me open and shut again. I looked over my shoulder. Harry's man was back, to tell him the money was where I'd said it was.

Then a mobile chimed in. It was Leroy's. He took the call and listened, saying next to nothing himself. Then he switched off and put the phone back in his pocket.

'They've got the kids, boss,' Leroy said quietly.

'It's your lucky day,' Harry told me, smiling happily now. 'Not my wife's, though.'

I tried not to show it but I felt dreadful. My hands had locked into fists but there was no point launching myself at Harry. The odds were hopeless. Guns were at the ready.

'You'd better look after them,' I told him.

He gave me a contemptuous glance and turned away.

Things speeded up after that. Harry got up and started issuing orders. He told Leroy to lock the old couple in a bedroom. As for me, I was ordered, at gunpoint, downstairs into a cellar. The door was slammed shut and locked. Five minutes later I heard vehicles leaving. I was still alive.

I gave it a minute or two. Then I started exploring. The cellar had a small window that opened partway. If it had not had stout iron bars embedded in concrete I might have thought of escaping that way. As it was, the locked door seemed the better prospect.

But that wasn't an easy option. The door was constructed of heavy timber. The lock looked pretty old and obsolete, but it was heavy duty. The door shuddered when I hit it with my shoulder and kicked it, but I soon realized I couldn't burst it open that way.

I tried levering it open with a length of wood. The wood snapped. The same thing

124

happened to an old spade I found and tried using.

I stepped back and caught my breath, wiped my forehead with the back of my hand. Then I looked for another route out of the cellar. I used a solid length of timber to attack the ceiling, hammering at the ends of a couple of boards until the nails sprang loose. I stood on a box and pushed the boards upwards until they broke away. Light flooded into the cellar. I widened the gap and pulled myself up into the kitchen.

After I had caught my breath and knocked the dust and cobwebs off, I went looking for Vlasta's parents. They were in the second bedroom I tried. The door wasn't locked, but it didn't need to be: they weren't going anywhere.

I grimaced and swore with rage, scarcely able to believe how much blood had leaked out of them. It was Leroy's doing. I knew that.

He had marched them in there, sat them down on the bed and cut their throats, probably so fast they didn't even see it coming. At least, I certainly hoped that was the case.

It was one more thing Leroy was going to pay for. I promised myself that.

16

On the drive back to Jetřichovice I tried to stick to the facts. Vlasta's parents were gone. I knew that. Harry had the kids, it seemed. As for Vlasta, I had no idea what had happened to her, and I didn't want to speculate. I would wait till I got there.

So I tried not to think. But I felt. Mostly I felt anger and guilt. I simply hadn't understood how resourceful and ruthless Harry and co. were. I had thought that by changing vehicles we had eliminated the possibility of being tracked. But I seemed to have got that wrong.

I'd also not reckoned with the sheer malevolence of Leroy. He was in a class of his own. There had been no reason to do anything to the old couple, and so far as I knew Harry had not ordered it, but he'd gone ahead anyway. So I'd got that wrong, too.

It was hard to believe now that I would find Vlasta alive. But I hoped I would, and I clung to that hope like a child to a teddy bear.

★ ★ ★

I parked the car under trees alongside the access track and approached the old mill on foot. I stood and watched for a while but the place was quiet. It wasn't a big building and we had seemed to be the only guests. The couple who owned and ran the guest house appeared to be out. At least, their car was gone. There was nobody around at all.

Better get on with it.

I waited a minute or two longer, listening to the hum of spring insects and the chatter of birds in the surrounding woodland. Then I broke cover and headed directly for the main door. It was open. The restaurant just inside was empty. A clock ticked. A refrigerator came on, making me jump. When I'd calmed down again, I wiped the sweat out of my eyes and got on with it.

The stone staircase was gloomy and silent. I made my way up it cautiously, keeping as much as possible to the shadows, avoiding the patches of sunlight penetrating the occasional tiny windows.

The corridor was different. Late sunlight poured through a big window at the western end and reached all the way along to the head of the stairs. There were no shadows to exploit here. I hesitated. The door to our room at the far end of the corridor was wide open. To reach it meant crossing a long, exposed stretch. At least the floor was tiled. No boards to creak and give warning.

I waited, listening and feeling for a threatening presence. Nothing. Get on with it! I made my way quickly and silently along the corridor. Just before I reached the door I paused again and glanced behind me. Still nothing. I crouched and swung into the room.

It was empty. There was no one here.

I stood still and let my eyes range around the room, absorbing, digesting. Then I saw the lump on one of the beds, covered by a quilt. I froze. It was what I had feared. It had to be Vlasta.

Feeling sick, I reluctantly made my way across the room. Without giving myself time to think, I pulled back the quilt to expose the body beneath.

It was Vlasta, face down.

I stared, noting the lack of blood, wondering if she had been strangled.

Then the body moved, turned on to its back and stared up at me with a tear-ravaged face.

★ ★ ★

She didn't want to talk. Perhaps couldn't. Not a word, for a long time. I held her for a while. Then I left her to it.

I hunted through their things, hers and the children's. They were all there, the backpacks and plastic bags I recognized. I tipped Vlasta's bag out on to a bed and pored through her bras and knickers, her jeans and a couple of dresses. Then I went through her make-up bag. There wasn't a lot of stuff. She travelled light, if you disregarded the small matter of a million quid in bank notes that she had set out with. Money like that with you, and you don't really need to take much else.

Petr's bag had spare jeans, too, and plenty of socks and pants. A red jumper. Pyjamas. A couple of soldiers and a dumper truck. But not what I was looking for.

I saw it as soon as I tipped Hannah's bag out. I didn't bother with her clothes or the Enid Blyton story book. Nor the toiletries. I went straight for the teddy bear.

It was one of those that you buy as an empty shell and then have filled and blown up until you've got the bear you always wanted. This one wasn't hard-packed and solid. More like a rag doll. I squeezed and soon found it, a hard lump in one leg. I took out my pocket knife and began to saw through the stitching around the foot.

I never heard her coming. She hit me hard,

coming from behind and hurling herself at me, screaming.

I dropped everything and fought to throw her off. She was strong and fought like a fury. I flattened her on the bed, and held her down. She spat at me. I held on and waited.

'What are you doing?' she hissed when she remembered it was no use screaming at me in Czech. 'You have destroyed my children. Now you destroy their possessions!'

By sheer weight and strength I pinned her down until I felt the fight go out of her. Then I let go and stepped back.

'Remember one thing, Vlasta,' I said wearily. 'Harry wanted the children badly. He won't harm them. He took them, but he won't harm them. Hang on to that thought.'

She turned her face away. It was more complicated than I had suggested but I didn't bother reminding her of the complication, the fact that the attack on the autobahn could have been fatal for us all.

'Feel this,' I instructed, pressing the teddy bear's leg into her hand. 'Feel it? That lump? I couldn't understand how they could have found you here. This is how.'

Her fingers reluctantly squeezed the teddy bear. I pulled it away from her, found my knife and completed opening the seam. I drew out the small metal object and held it in front of her eyes.

She stared at it.

'It's a tracker bug. I assumed it was in the car, but it wasn't. It was right here, with us all the time.'

She sat up and took it from me. She examined it.

'So Hannah brought it?' she said at length.

'It wasn't her fault. She didn't know. But, yes, she did. Maybe there was one in the car, as well.'

It got easier after that. She began to talk to me. She told me what had happened. It was a simple enough story. Three men had overpowered her. They told her to stay where she was if she didn't want any harm to come to the children when they left.

'They'll be all right,' I said again.

Then I told her about her parents. Might as well get it over with. She collapsed again, of course. Blamed herself, as well she might. It actually *was* her fault it had all happened. But what choice had she had? I told her she had done what she had had to do. She had tried to make the best of a bad situation, and that was that. Now we had to live with the consequences.

I left her for a while. I went outside and breathed in the scent of the forest. I wandered, not far but just to let it all settle. Then I went back inside and climbed the old staircase again, and returned along the ceramic-tiled corridor to our room.

'What can we do now?' Vlasta asked when I went back inside.

I was relieved. She was back with me, her pieces put back together again.

★   ★   ★

To me, it was pretty straightforward. I wouldn't rest until we got the kids back. But there was a puzzle to be resolved, too. At least one.

'Harry's got the money and the kids,' I said. 'He's got most of what he wanted. But he hasn't got you. Why not? They could have taken you as well.'

She shrugged. 'Not enough space in their car, maybe. Or Harry doesn't want me back.'

Oh, no! Not good enough, Vlasta.

Then she threw in another complication uninvited. 'Anyway, they are not his children. They are mine only.'

At last! Vlasta confirming what Bill Peart had already told me.

'They're not Harry's?'

She shook her head. 'They were born before I met Harry. They came with me to England.'

I struggled with that one. Harry must have

really fancied her, baggage and all. How things can change!

'So why did he want them back so badly?'

She shrugged again. 'To hurt me.'

That made sense, of a sort. But I was still left wondering why they hadn't lifted Vlasta as well as the children. Harry could have done much more to hurt her. Too simple, perhaps. Maybe Harry liked to stretch things out, extend the pain, by leaving her in limbo.

If we'd still had the money bag, another possible explanation could have been that the kids were a bargaining chip. But Harry had the money now. Vlasta had nothing left to bargain with, did she?

'Where could they have taken Hannah and Petr? Any ideas?'

She just shook her head. She had none to offer.

'Back to England?'

'I don't know,' she said. 'I really don't know where they are.'

I could believe that, at least.

One certainty I had was that we would get the kids back. I would go to the ends of the earth for them, if necessary, but somehow I would find them and return them to their mother.

And I would pay Leroy back. That was another certainty.

17

'I hate him!' Vlasta said bitterly. 'I hate him with all my heart for what he has done to me, and to others.'

I had gathered that. I didn't respond. I was just happy she was no longer a quivering heap of jelly.

My focus was on what next. Where the hell were Harry and the children? Where would he have taken them?

Vlasta was chuntering on about Harry and his trafficking of women. I kept one ear on her as I wandered over to the window. When she had calmed down a bit we would get out of here. There was no point staying.

'And now he wants to kill you?' I said, wondering why it hadn't happened already.

She shrugged. 'He wants me to continue doing what I have been doing for him — and I won't! So now he has the children, he thinks he can make me do what he wants.'

That was different. Perhaps he no longer wanted to kill her, after all? Perhaps he never had.

'Oh, yes! He wants to kill me. If he can, he

will. It is a matter of honour for him, because I left him.'

So we were back to our starting point. He would kill her if he could.

But I didn't know what to believe now. Where was truth? Did Harry want to force her to continue doing what she no longer wanted to do, or did he want to kill her? Or would he just give her another beating? That wasn't a wonderful prospect, but it was a bit better than the original alternative.

I let her go on, no longer really listening. I waited for her to get it all off her chest. I stared out at the forest, which came up close to the old mill, so close I could reach out and grasp bunches of leaves from the nearest enormous beech tree. Beyond that, beyond the dappled light reaching through the beech canopy, it was darker. The conifers, spruce and fir, stood tall and dense. And dark and quiet. Not much bird chatter now. As if the forest was settling down for the night.

Vlasta said, 'You don't know what it is like.'

'No,' I said automatically. 'I don't. You're right.'

A blackbird streaked through the trees, uttering a long, drawn-out cackle that brought me out of my reverie.

'Quick! Get your things.'

My bag was still packed and zipped tight. I grabbed it.

'What is it?' Vlasta demanded.

'They're coming back. We've got to get out. Quick!'

It wasn't certain. All that had happened was that a bird had given its warning call. But I felt it, and as soon as I felt it, it seemed right. It was what they would do. They were returning to complete the job. We had to get out.

Vlasta was good. She didn't argue. She didn't stop to pack. She just grabbed a small backpack, pushed a few things into it and came to me in the doorway. I hustled her along the corridor. At the top of the stairs I paused and held up a hand to warn her to keep quiet. I listened. And heard the creak of the front door opening. Nothing else. Just that. It was enough.

I touched Vlasta lightly on the arm and moved back. She followed. The main staircase was out. So was the fire escape. But there had to be another way out of there.

At the far end of the corridor I opened a door. A very constricted spiral staircase appeared. The servants' stairs. From the old days. Good enough for us.

I descended cautiously, with Vlasta close behind. Like being inside a vertical tube.

Curved sandstone wall, cold to the touch. Well-worn stone steps, illuminated by shafts of light from occasional tiny apertures. An iron handrail on the inside curve. No sounds from below.

I kept going. We emerged into a cellar, a stone-walled cellar with an archway leading into a vast kitchen, now unused. Stone troughs and a huge fireplace in which you could have roasted a pig, or perhaps an ox. The air was cool, the place silent. I pointed to the way out and made for a big double door.

The huge bolts were well greased. I drew them back without making a sound. I turned the big key in the massive lock slowly. It made no noise. I eased the door open an inch or two. Light flooded in. And the evening sounds of the forest.

I opened the door further. No one was in sight. We were, I realized, at the back of the building. The ground was overgrown with shrubs and bramble. If there had ever been a proper path, it was no longer visible. I led Vlasta out and gently closed the door after us. Then we moved along the wall.

A man came round the corner of the building just before we reached it. He was as surprised as us, perhaps more so — he had no reason to be cautious. He raised the pistol he was carrying. But I had reacted first. I hit him in the belly. He went down. I chopped at him until he was still. Then I picked up the gun, checked it and kept it ready.

No one else appeared. I glanced quickly round the corner of the building and led Vlasta out into the forest. We had to get away from there as quickly as we could.

I didn't think twice about the car. It would have been spotted. And perhaps guarded. It wasn't worth the risk. Instead, we took a direct line into the forest, moving cautiously until we hit a path and could move faster.

Vlasta broke the silence. 'We were lucky.'

Perhaps, I thought, but we weren't out of it yet.

★   ★   ★

After a couple of miles we reached the outskirts of a small village. There were not many people about but there were a couple of dozen cars parked outside a small hotel that obviously had a popular restaurant. We could hear people enjoying themselves inside. Many of the cars had German licence plates. We took one of them, a rather nice old Audi. The owner had conveniently left a window open to allow the heat to dissipate. So starting it up took even fewer seconds than it would have done anyway.

'Get in,' I said.

Vlasta had been watching with amazement. 'We can't . . . '

'Get in!'

She got in.

I drove quietly away, disturbing no one. Once we were out of sight I put my foot down. The car went well. I had picked a good one.

'Where are we going?' Vlasta asked, still apparently shocked by being party to car theft. 'We're going home,' I told her.

18

To me, it was simple. There was nothing here for Harry George now. No reason to extend his stay. He had the kids. Even more important, he had the money. He didn't have his wife, but there were others looking for her. He didn't need to be here himself. Finally, he was vulnerable here. This wasn't his territory, and, with the exception of Leroy, they weren't his men who were doing the hunting; they were Czech speakers. He would be better off at home.

I explained all this to Vlasta in the hours it took us to drive to Prague, dump the car in the airport car park, buy tickets and scramble aboard an Easyjet flight to Manchester shortly before it took off. I explained it all but I don't know how interested she was. There were only two things bothering her. I could do nothing immediately about the first, the children, and she knew it. The second was a different matter.

'You shouldn't have taken the car,' she said bitterly more than once. 'It is not ours.'

'We had to get away from there.'

'It makes all Czechs look bad. The

Germans will think worse of us.'

I contented myself with wondering how good it would have looked to German visitors to find two more dead bodies in the Czech countryside: hers and mine.

* * *

We hired a car at Manchester Airport and were back at Risky Point in time for breakfast. The cottage was still standing, I was relieved to see. No mysterious fire had removed it from the face of the earth.

I waved to Jimmy Mack, who was leaning on his garden wall, and ushered Vlasta indoors. I was running on empty now; the adrenaline had just about all left my system. Jimmy would have to wait for an explanation as to why I had not taken his advice with regard to yet another woman.

I showed Vlasta into the spare bedroom and dumped a load of bedding on her. 'That's it,' I told her. 'Get some sleep. We'll talk later.'

'What . . . ?'

'Later, Vlasta. Not now. Neither of us is any shape to talk sense at the moment.'

Reluctantly, she turned away and stared despondently at the heap of bedding. I left her to it.

For me, at least, sleep came easily. Nothing was urgent or important enough to get in the way for even a moment.

★   ★   ★

It was mid afternoon when I surfaced. I lay there for a few moments, luxuriating in the sense of security and wellness that comes from being somewhere safe where you feel happy and content.

Then I remembered Hannah and Petr. Soon afterwards I felt pangs of hunger and knew it was time to face the world.

Vlasta had beaten me to it. Washed and dressed, I went downstairs to find my kitchen table set for two, and food awaiting me. Vlasta had ransacked the cupboards and freezer, and come up with enough to satisfy a lot more than two people. Bread, cheese, eggs, sliced meat, sliced peppers and tomatoes . . . I hadn't realized there was so much stuff there.

Vlasta was outside. She heard me coming and came back in with a smile.

'Did you sleep?' I asked her.

'A little,' she conceded.

She looked tired but in control. She seemed fine. Except she was anxious about the food she had prepared. Was it enough?

I laughed. 'Wonderful! Come on. Let's dig in.'

* ★ ★ ★

'What do we do now, Frank?'

I wished she wouldn't ask me questions like that, as I didn't like lying to her. She was so needy I found it hard to cope with her questions.

She wanted her kids back. Maybe the million quid, too. I reckoned she could kiss the money goodbye but I was hopeful and determined about the kids. I would look for them, but in my own way. I didn't want Vlasta with me. Nor did I want to have to explain to her how difficult it was going to be, let alone what the chances of success were.

'Vlasta, I'm going to do the best I can, but right now I can't answer many of your questions. You're going to have to live with that. I'm sorry.'

She looked ready to argue, but she stopped herself in time. 'OK, Frank. I know you will do your best. I will try to be patient.'

'Thank you.'

'So today?'

'Today I'm going to see my neighbour, Jimmy Mack. I need to find out what's been going on here, if anything. Then I'm going into town to ask other people some questions.'

'Can I come with you?'

I shook my head. 'Better not, Vlasta. People might recognize you and decide they don't want to answer questions about Harry George if his wife is standing next to me.'

That wasn't the whole story, but she accepted it. I was relieved. I needed to be able to do things my way, without having to worry about her or what she thought.

'Come on,' I said. 'Let's go and see Jimmy.'

★   ★   ★

Plenty had been going on in my absence.

'First, your policeman friend came.'

'Detective Inspector Bill Peart?'

'Is that his name? Big fellow. Losing his hair. Worried looking.'

I chuckled. 'That's him.'

'Well, he came and said there was a possibility that some gangster types might be sniffing around. I told him I'd soon see them off. I've been here a long time, I told him. Nobody frightens me.

'He seemed to have his doubts. Left me one of them mobile phone things, and said to just press this button if anything seemed to be going on at your place.'

I found myself blessing Bill Peart. Why hadn't I thought of that?

'So nothing happened?'

'Not at first, no.'

He was looking now at Vlasta, weighing her up. She hadn't said anything since I had introduced them. He didn't know what to make of her.

'Vlasta?' he said. 'What kind of name is that? Russian?'

He wasn't far out, I thought with a smile.

'Czech,' Vlasta said. 'I am Czech.'

'Oh? Czechoslovakia, eh?'

'No,' Vlasta said impatiently. 'Czech. I am from the Czech Republic.'

'It used to be part of Czechoslovakia,' I said gently. I could see they were becoming impatient with each other.

'Get away?' Jimmy said reflectively. 'There was some of them people around here in 1956, after the Revolution. They were in a camp at Marske.'

'They were Hungarians,' I intervened, before it could get completely out of hand.

'That's right. Like I said.'

Vlasta was indignant now. 'They are different to us. Hungarians? They are from another country!'

'Oh?' Jimmy gave me a wink.

'Come on, you daft old bugger,' I said

wearily. 'What happened after Bill Peart came to see you?'

Vlasta was about to continue the debate but I grimaced to shut her up. She turned away in apparent disgust.

'A couple of days later a van turned up. Two or three blokes were in it. They stopped outside your place and started unloading petrol cans. A couple of them had seen me, and came over here. I could see they were a bad lot. They had no business being here at all. One of them — '

'So what did you do?'

'I pressed the button.'

'And?'

'That fellow, that friend of yours, came on. So I told him. He said they'd be here in five minutes. Maybe less. Not to worry. Just take the photos, and sit tight.'

'Photos? What photos?'

'Didn't I mention that? He left me this camera, as well as the phone. Told me to take pictures — point and press the button, that's all I had to do — and then chuck it over the cliff.'

I just stared at him. This was becoming the most extraordinary conversation I'd ever had with Jimmy Mack.

'So they couldn't take the camera off me,' Jimmy explained patiently. 'I had to chuck it over the edge, out of harm's way. They would be able to recover it later. He said it was waterproof and shockproof.'

I nodded. It was making more sense now. Clever Bill Peart.

'So what happened?'

'I made sure they saw me taking pictures. Then I did what your mate had said. I chucked it over the edge.'

I found myself thinking he was lucky he hadn't been made to follow the camera.

'Then what?'

'I told them I'd called the police, who were on their way. And I'd taken their pictures. So they'd better be off.'

'They were happy with that?'

'Not really, no. But what were they going to do? They pushed me around a bit.' Jimmy pointed to a new bruise I'd seen on his face. 'Then they went back to the van. Put the petrol cans away and drove off.'

'Petrol cans?' Vlasta said, puzzled.

'To start the fire,' Jimmy explained.

'Fire?'

'To burn the cottage down.'

Vlasta looked horrified, as well she might. The ramifications of that simple little job she had offered me in the beginning just kept on getting ever more tangled.

'Did the police come?' I asked.

Jimmy nodded. 'I was surprised how quick they got here. Two big Volvos. I told them what had happened. Then they took off after the van.'

'What about the camera?' Vlasta asked, recovering and proving she had been following the conversation.

'They soon got that,' Jimmy said with satisfaction. 'Where I'd chucked it, they didn't even need a diver to recover it. A man just roped down the cliff and picked it up.'

'Thanks, Jimmy. You did well,' I told him. 'How are you feeling now?'

'Never better,' he said with a twisted grin.

I doubted that but I let it go.

I told him we'd be there for a little while now. A few days, at least.

'Good,' he said. 'So you'll have time to tell me what's going on?'

I grinned, made a sort of promise and ushered Vlasta away.

'He is not so stupid as he seems, I think,' Vlasta confided as we walked back towards my place.

'Jimmy? No, he's not stupid at all.'

'In my country, in villages,' she added, 'the old people always used *husa* — the goose — to guard their houses and gardens. They are better than dogs.'

'Oh?'

'But you don't need such creatures. You have Jimmy. Am I right?'

I laughed. I didn't need to say another word.

19

Leroy waited until the others had moved on. He wasn't going with them. They had been his to command for a while, but he wasn't one of them. Besides, his agenda was different to theirs.

He made the call.

'It's done,' he said.

'No problems?'

'No problems. You've got what you wanted.'

Afterwards, he did some more waiting, thinking it all through again. When he was sure he had thought of everything he left to embark on the next stage of his journey. No turning back now. Not ever. He was on his own.

20

Harry's club, *Aphrodite's,* was located in an old building that had once been known to generations of Redcar people as 'The Rock Factory'. I could recall seeing the long strips of multi-striped, hard candy with 'Redcar' running all the way through them in the open section on the ground floor at the front of the building. It was hard now to believe that once there had been sufficient demand for seaside rock to require a dedicated building of this size. Hard, too, to believe that this undistinguished building had more recently come to the notice of some east European mafia-style gang.

I parked the car on the prom and wandered along a little way, giving Harry's building the eye. At this time of day, late afternoon, nothing much was happening. One or two people who looked like staff came and went. A small group of cleaners left. The lull before the storm. Preparations being made for the evening. Always assuming it was a club that still attracted enough punters to justify switching on the lights.

The front of the building, facing the sea,

was smart and bright enough. When all the neon lit up, it would be even brighter. Just now, though, the seductive lady in chiffon and gauze could only be seen in dull outline, but BAR was lit up in blue and yellow. I decided to check on the daytime revellers.

The doors were open. A small lounge bar was illuminated, and the young guy putting away clean glasses was keen to serve me — anyone! — with anything to break the monotony.

'I'll just have a coffee,' I told him.

He shrugged and said, 'Sure.'

As he went to work on the big machine, getting the steam pulsing, I added, 'I came in because I wanted to see Harry George. Is he around?'

'Nope.'

He poured my espresso and brought it over, along with sachets of milk powder and sugar.

'When is it best to catch him?'

He looked me over, shook his head and said scornfully, 'You want to see Harry George? Really?'

'I do.'

'Phone for an appointment,' he said, turning away.

'Thanks.'

The coffee wasn't bad, and I wasn't upset

about the attitude or the advice. I was only here to see what the place was like.

'Has he been around lately?' I asked.

The guy just looked at me.

'I heard he was abroad somewhere.'

'What do you want?'

'To see Harry George.'

I could see he was getting annoyed now. 'Finish your coffee,' he suggested, 'and get out of here. On second thoughts, just get out!'

I tut-tutted as he pulled my cup away. 'You realize you're soon going to have a new boss? You should be careful how you treat customers like me. You have no idea who I am. What did you say your name was?'

He was mad now, but he was also worried. He didn't know what to do. As I'd pointed out, he didn't know who I was. But temper, fury, had got the better of him.

'Touch that,' I warned, as he reached under the bar for something, probably his weapon of choice, a baseball bat, maybe, 'and you're not going to live long.'

I took the automatic out of my pocket and worked the slide. No way was I going anywhere unarmed now. I'd recently met too many dangerous people.

He stopped and took stock. 'What do you want?' he said again, this time in a calmer tone.

'I want to see Harry. You sure he's not here?'

He shook his head.

'Leroy?'

'He's not here either.'

'They're abroad, I hear.'

'Maybe.'

He straightened up and moved back, as if getting out of reach would also put him beyond the range of bullets.

I nodded. 'Stay cool,' I said. 'I'm going to look round.'

★ ★ ★

The lights were on everywhere, proving there wasn't much to see. Late at night, or in the early hours, with the lights turned down, and if you were full of drink or coke, or whatever drug was fashionable with clubbers these days, *Aphrodite's* would no doubt look different, but just then it looked like an empty factory. There wasn't even any music, if you discounted a vacuum cleaner droning in the distance. Just a big empty space with a dance area in the middle and seating cubicles around the edges, and a pervasive, overall smell of dirt and sweat. Not a patch on Vegas.

Upstairs there were offices, all of them unoccupied. Some had filing cabinets and desks. Others had low lounge chairs around a low table, where businessmen no doubt talked business and perhaps hatched plots or paid for lap dances. There was nothing to interest me at all.

'Can I help you?'

I had just come out of one office and was about to set off down a corridor leading to stairs and the exit. The big guy who had asked the question was standing in the way.

'Probably not,' I said with a smile. 'I'm looking for Harry, but I guess he's not here.'

'You're looking for Harry?'

'That's right.'

'Harry being?'

'The boss man. I want to talk to him.'

'And you thought you'd just wander through private property till you found him?'

He was surprisingly well spoken. Big, but smooth. Not a bouncer. Not a Leroy either. More like a manager type.

'I don't like your tone,' I told him. 'Who are you, anyway?'

'I run this place. You'd better get out before I have you thrown out.'

The bad moment was past. He wasn't going to shoot me.

'I'm leaving anyway. When I see him, I'll tell Harry how friendly you've been.'

'Crap.'

'I'll also tell your new boss. He'll want to know who's worth keeping on when Harry moves out.'

That shut him up. He followed me along the corridor and watched me go down the stairs and hit the exit. I hadn't learned much, but I had learned that if *Aphrodite's* was still Harry George's, he no longer had much to do with it. I'd also learned it wasn't much of a business any more. The place was on its uppers.

More to the point, there were no children there. Hannah and Petr were elsewhere.

★ ★ ★

'Where did you live?'

Vlasta looked at me suspiciously.

'You and Harry, and the children. Where's home. Where *was* home?'

She shrugged. 'There is a house, where we lived. Not Harry. For a long time he was not there much.'

I was trying to be patient. Her life had come apart. Parents dead. Kids gone. Husband responsible for it all. She was in a mess. But it was still hard work getting her to tell me anything.

'OK,' I said. 'There were no signs of him at the club. Where — '

156

'The club? You have been there?'

I nodded.

She appeared about to remonstrate with me, as if I had no right going there without her permission or company. Then she shrugged.

'The next obvious place to look is the house where you lived. Where is it?'

'I will come with you,' she said firmly.

'Let's go.'

'Five minutes? I must tell Jimmy.'

'Tell him what?'

'That I won't be able to go fishing with him this evening.'

I shook my head and smiled to myself as she set off for the other cottage. It sounded as if she and Jimmy had struck up a friendship. I was pleased. Life might be easier for me in future.

True to precedent, Vlasta didn't tell me where the house was, still less the address. Instead, she gave me directions along the way. Somehow I managed not to be irritated.

So we headed off into the hills, past New Marske and Skelton, out near Guisborough. There, we came to a hamlet with a big house at one end, a house surrounded by ancient sycamores, big laurel bushes and acres of lawn. It was built of the very red local sandstone, in a well proportioned mid-nineteenth-century way. Once it had been a rectory, apparently in the days when rectors had big families and many servants. More recently, it had been home to Vlasta and Hannah and Petr, and occasionally to Harry George as well.

No cars were parked on the gravelled forecourt. No windows I could see were open. The big front door was firmly shut. I sensed abandonment.

Vlasta had lost the keys she had been carrying with her, but she knew where there was a spare set hanging up in the potting shed next to the big greenhouse.

'My plants!' she exclaimed, seeing the dead and dying courgettes and cucumbers, lettuce and tomatoes. 'There is nobody to water them.'

I said nothing. I was happy for her to be distracted from thoughts of the children, who clearly neither of us expected to find here.

Vlasta opened the front door and we stepped inside. You can always tell when a house is unoccupied. However much furniture is in it, the place has a still quality and a stale smell. A house needs people to give it life. This one didn't have it.

We walked through the downstairs rooms. Everything was tidy. Nothing was out of place. A note on the hall table told us that Mrs Empson had been, as usual, to clean, and would not be back again until she was informed that someone was back in residence.

'They are not here,' Vlasta said.

'No.'

Looking desolate, she added, 'And they have not been here.'

That was as clear to me as it was to Vlasta. We looked upstairs but saw nothing in any of the bedrooms to make us change our minds. Neither Harry nor the children had been back to the house since the day Vlasta had left it.

'Do you want to stay here?' I asked.

She shook her head.

'It's a nice house.'

She agreed but I could see her point when she said, 'It is a nice house but it is not a home. It is not my home.'

Close to tears, she added, 'My home is where my children are, but I had such hopes when I first came here. It seemed perfect.'

I didn't want her being sentimental or nostalgic on me. There was too much to do. 'Collect any clothes and little things you might need, and let's get out of here.'

'What will we do now, Frank?' she asked, looking tearful and dejected.

'Go back to Risky Point,' I said, 'and then think about where to look next for the children.'

I wasn't too disappointed. I hadn't really expected to find Hannah and Petr, or Harry for that matter, at either the club or the family house. But they were both places I had needed to see and cross off the list. I had some ideas about what to do next but I wasn't about to share them with Vlasta. My hope was I could dump her on Jimmy Mack, and give myself some slack to search unencumbered. Vlasta wasn't made for doing what I suspected I would have to do now.

21

Late as it was, Bill Peart was waiting for me when we got back to Risky Point. He was talking to Jimmy Mack outside Jimmy's cottage. I let Vlasta into the house and waited for Bill to come over.

'You must have a big overtime budget in your department,' I said as he approached.

'You'd think so, wouldn't you.'

'Bring your tackle?'

He shook his head. 'It's you I wanted to see, not giant waves and big fish.'

'Pity. I owe you a good fish. I appreciate what you did for us, Bill. In fact, I don't know how you managed it. You didn't have much time to get here when Jimmy called.'

He shrugged. 'For once, our interests coincided.'

I interpreted what he was saying. They must have been lined up to move in on Harry and his boys as soon as they stepped out of line. Jimmy had been lucky. So had I.

'Was that Mrs George I saw going into your house?'

I nodded. 'That's her. Do you want to meet her?'

161

'I need to. But I'll have a word with you first, Frank.'

I motioned towards the driftwood table and sat down with him.

'There's a few things you need to know, Bill.'

'Oh?'

'We've just come back from the Czech Republic, Vlasta's homeland.'

'From whence you phoned me?'

I nodded. 'We encountered Harry George there. We did a deal with him. Some money got exchanged. But he out-manoeuvred us and took the kids.'

'Leroy with him?'

I nodded. 'A few others, as well. Locals, I believe.' I sighed and decided to spill the rest of it. 'They murdered Vlasta's parents.'

He looked at me bleakly and said, 'Boy, you really got out-manoeuvred.'

'Yeah.' I grimaced. 'Vlasta and the kids were my priority. I was concentrating on keeping them alive.'

I shrugged and added, 'Then things took an unexpected turn. I don't think it was Harry's doing. It was Leroy. That bastard's a headcase!'

Bill gave me his stern, official stare. 'You never thought of the police? They must have them over there. More than us, probably.

162

They must be teeming with them.'

I shook my head. 'Vlasta wouldn't hear of it. And she was my client. Still is, as far as I know.'

'What about the law, Frank?'

I was getting tired of being on the defensive and being made to feel guilty. 'The law, Bill? What about it? And which law? Whose law?'

'Murder must be the same kind of crime over there as it is here. They're in the EU now, aren't they?'

'Probably.'

I let it rest a moment and then said, 'Harry's got the kids, Bill. They mean the world to Vlasta. And they're not his.'

Bill shuffled uncomfortably and said, 'Have you got any coffee in the house? It's time I brought Mrs George into the discussion.'

I raised my eyebrows.

'I don't know who has the kids now, Frank, but it's certainly not Harry George. Come on. Let's go inside.'

★ ★ ★

Vlasta was visibly on edge when I introduced Bill. Conditioning, I suppose. Her experience of police officers must have made her that way.

'He's a friend, Vlasta,' I told her. 'Not just a cop.'

She did her best to relax. 'I am pleased to meet you, Mr Peart.'

Bill ducked his head in acknowledgement. He was pretty stiff, too. It wasn't just Vlasta. You'd think he wasn't used to meeting strippers and gangsters' wives.

'I have some news, Mrs George,' he said. 'Sad news. We've been notified by Czech police that they have found the body of your husband.'

Vlasta was stunned. Me, too. That wasn't what I had expected to hear.

'He is dead?' Vlasta said faintly.

'I'm afraid so.'

'Then what about my children?' she whispered with dread.

'I don't know. The Czech police have not given us any information about them.'

To me, that seemed good news. Relatively good news, at least. Vlasta seemed to think so, too. She drew herself up and thanked Bill for delivering the message. Then she looked at me and announced that she was very tired. Would I mind if . . . ?

'Not at all,' I assured her. 'Go ahead. You know where everything is.'

I put the kettle on and started to make coffee. Bill stood against the window and

164

stared out at the sea. By tacit agreement we said nothing more until the coffee was made. Perhaps he was tired. I know I was. We both needed a stimulant. I opened a cupboard and took out a bottle of Famous Grouse and a couple of glasses.

'This view,' he said, shaking his head, as I planted everything on the table. 'I would never get to work if I had this to look at every morning.'

'It's hard,' I agreed.

He turned reluctantly and made his way over to join me at the table.

'Your news wasn't that bad,' I said quietly. 'It would have been better if they had found the kids — found them alive — but Vlasta won't shed many tears over Harry.'

'No, I don't suppose she will. She must be tough as old boots to have been married to him.'

That was one way of putting it. Myself, I still wasn't sure what the truth was. Tough sometimes, vulnerable others. And a good actress. Not forgetting that. No wonder she had been a top-class performer. No wonder Harry had wanted her.

I poured two glasses of scotch and slid one over to stand alongside Bill's coffee mug. He nodded his thanks. We touched glasses. I took a sip from mine.

'The Czech police made no mention of the kids?'

He shook his head.

'How did Harry die?'

'They said his throat was cut.'

I grimaced with surprise. 'That sounds like Leroy.'

'Possibly.'

I mulled it over. The information made little sense to me. 'But Leroy is, was, Harry's man.'

'Was he really?'

'Well . . . I thought he was. He seemed to be.'

'There you go, jumping to conclusions.'

The obvious conclusion, if indeed Leroy had done it, was that he had been working for the other side, Harry's new business partners. Either all along or because he had changed sides when he saw the way the wind was blowing.

'Maybe it wasn't Leroy?' I said without much conviction.

'That, too,' Bill admitted. He yawned and emptied his glass. 'Anyway, it's not our case. Maybe the Czechs will get to the bottom of it.'

And maybe Harry will come back to life, I thought, cut throat and all.

'What will you do now, Frank?'

I shook my head. 'I'll wait until Vlasta has got some sleep. Me, too. Then I'll talk to her.'

'What will you do now, Frank?' he repeated, staring at me.

I stared back. 'Find the kids,' I said eventually.

He nodded and pushed his chair back to stand up. 'Let me know how it goes.'

On the way out, he said, 'We'll want to see Mrs George again. Officially There'll be pieces to pick up, and there's still the children. Are they British citizens?'

I shrugged.

'Well, if we can help her, we will. But in any case we need to go through a few things with her.'

'Sure. Thanks a lot, Bill.'

'Take care,' he added as he headed out into the night.

It seemed good advice, and well meant. I waited outside until I saw him turn onto the main road.

22

I wondered what had woken me. It was still dark. Even without glancing at my watch on the bedside table I knew it was still the small hours. Maybe two or three. At this time of year it was light soon after four.

I lay still, concentrating, gathering myself, preparing. My heart beat was rising. I kept perfectly still, but ready to launch into action.

Then I heard Vlasta say something. Not much. A few words I couldn't make out. Some of the tension left me. I could tell she was on the phone, responding. An incoming call must have woken me, as well as her.

I lay there a few moments longer. Then I got up and put on my shorts. I headed for the door.

Vlasta was in her room. I listened outside the door. She didn't say much. Brief, monosyllabic responses mostly. And what she did say was not in English. Czech, presumably.

I left her to it and went downstairs. I put the kettle on, in the usual automatic way. I was awake now and it was something to do.

Half past three, I noted from the kitchen clock. Already a patch of sky in the east was lighter. Another half hour and there would come that soft, grey, half-light you get just before the day breaks. A good hunting time, and a time to hide.

The kettle rumbled to a conclusion and I heard the click as it switched itself off. I reached for a mug. Then I heard Vlasta descending the stairs and reached for a second mug.

'Coffee?' I asked without looking round.

'Yes, please.'

I made the coffee and turned round to hand Vlasta hers. For a moment I paused. She wasn't dressed in much, just a T-shirt that covered very little and emphasized her breasts. She was staring at me, but not with what had briefly crossed my mind. She looked scared.

'Who was it?'

'It was them.'

I knew who she meant. She didn't need to spell it out.

'Do they have the children?'

She nodded, and looked even more hopeless.

'Sit down, Vlasta.' I took her by the arm and gently steered her into a chair. I put a mug of coffee in front of her and sat down across the table from her. 'So what do they want?'

'They said I am now the owner of Harry's business and properties. Harry is dead, and I am his wife. So now I am the owner.'

She looked at me questioningly. I nodded. 'Technically, legally, that's true. I doubt if Harry anticipated this situation. So he won't have made any other arrangements.'

'They said I am to sign everything over to them — the businesses and the properties. They will arrange this with lawyers. And they will hold the children until I sign the documents.'

How very law abiding! It was extraordinary. Who the hell were these people?

'Who are they?'

She shrugged. 'I don't know much.'

'Vlasta! Cut it out. You do know something.'

'I know I will not see the children again unless I do what they say,' she said defiantly.

'Maybe not even then, Vlasta, unless we do something. Come on! Who are they?'

It was a big struggle for her. But she was alone. She needed me, or someone, on her side.

'They are Slovaks.'

'From Slovakia?'

'Yes.'

'Not your country?'

She shook her head. 'When I was young it was all one country, but not now. Now Slovakia is a foreign country. They are from there.'

Something didn't add up, puzzled me. How the hell had Harry George ever got involved with these people?

'Do you know them?'

She shrugged. 'Not really.'

That was enough for me.

'So where are they based?'

'Bratislava, maybe. I don't know.'

She did know. I was sure of that. But I didn't press her. It wasn't the time.

'That the capital?'

'Yes.'

They probably were there, in that case. Powerful gangs like big cities, and need them.

'So they are going to give you documents to sign. And until then, you must wait?'

She nodded.

'Where? Where must you wait?'

She looked startled. 'I don't know.'

'Did you tell them where you are now?'

'No.'

'That's OK. As long as they have your phone number they can reach you. They will tell you where to be.'

My guess was that nothing was going to

happen for a little while. They would have to get a lawyer to sort out with his English equivalent what needed doing, and then actually do it. We had a few days. Possibly more. At least, I had. What I had in mind wasn't going to involve Vlasta very much. I needed to park her.

I stood up and walked over to the window. It was light now. Once again, day had come. Soon, there would be sun, too.

'It's going to be a nice day,' I said over my shoulder.

I heard her get up. Her chair squeaked on the wooden floor. Then her arms went round me. She held on tight.

'Hold me,' she whispered. 'I'm scared.'

So I did. I held her close, and felt the heat of her through the thin fabric of her T-shirt. She buried her face in my chest. I felt her breasts pressing against me, and the hardness of her nipples. Then the inevitable happened, and she felt it. She reached for me, and I grew bigger. She pulled away and led me back up the stairs. I went willingly, desperate to have her wrapped round me.

⋆　⋆　⋆

Afterwards she said, 'What will we do now?'

Face more complications, I thought. But

172

the heat and the passion had not gone. We needed each other, in all sorts of ways, and for now we were one.

'We have a little time,' I said. 'It will be a few days before they contact you again. Maybe longer. Legal matters can't be rushed.

'I think you should stay here and wait for them to call. You'll be safe enough here. Safer than at Harry's house anyway. Jimmy will keep an eye out for you, and he has a good link to Bill Peart.'

'So I will stay here? It is safe here — for me? What about you, Frank?'

'I will be here, too, some of the time. But I have things to do. Don't worry about me.'

I couldn't tell her I was going to look for the children. She would want to come with me. I didn't want that. I was better on my own. She would just get in the way, make things more complicated.

'You'll be fine,' I added. 'Don't worry. Just remember: they need you. Without you, there's no possibility of them taking Harry's businesses over legally. And because they need you, they will look after the children.'

She seemed persuaded — for now. Conversation ceased. We slept. Wrapped in each other's arms we slept until the sun was high.

23

There were things for me to think about. There were things that bothered me. Beyond the obvious. I thought about them as I prepared breakfast, having left Vlasta asleep in bed.

Vlasta knew more about the Slovak crew than she was saying. That much was obvious. I suspected she had been some sort of go-between. How else could they and Harry have ever met up? Slovakia wasn't exactly on the map for provincial British criminals.

That thought raised the question of what had been in it for Vlasta. The answer I very quickly came up with was hard for me to accept. The woman I had just bedded didn't seem like a stone-cold killer. Surely all this hadn't been engineered just to remove her husband?

Money, then? Well, maybe. Her grabbing of Harry's money bag indicated she wasn't oblivious to the attractions of hard cash.

Other interesting questions included: Whose side had Leroy been on, Harry's or the Slovaks'? And was he really the one who had taken out Harry?

Finally — for now — where were the kids?

In relation to that last one, there were a few points that had occurred to me. For example, Vlasta still had their passports. I'd seen them. That being the case, how likely was it that the children had been taken across international boundaries? It would be hard, at a moment's notice, to take them through airports. Not so hard, though, to take them across borders by road vehicle — or on foot.

But, all in all, I reckoned there was a good chance they were still either in the Czech Republic or on the Slovaks' home ground, Slovakia. Much easier to hide them there than somewhere new, and there was no need to take them anywhere else.

I had another thought. Who had identified Harry's body? Bill Peart had not told me that. So what proof was there that Harry really was dead? A faked death would have been a good way for Harry to disappear with the kids and the money, especially if the business was going down the tubes. The more I thought about it, the more I liked that idea.

* * *

When I phoned him, Bill Peart said he didn't know who had identified the body.

'You don't know?'

'I can find out, I suppose. Do you want me to?'

'It seems like a good idea. I'm surprised you didn't think of it before I did.'

The phone went dead. I deduced that I had outstayed my CID favourite-visitors welcome.

★   ★   ★

Vlasta was on edge, but she knew she had to wait. That was all she could do until the Slovaks had the legal documents to put in front of her.

Meanwhile, there were things I wanted to know but couldn't ask about directly. I didn't want to disclose too much of my thinking.

Sitting outside the cottage with her, I mused about the documents she would have to sign. 'What other businesses did Harry have, in addition to the club?'

'Many things.' Vlasta shrugged. 'I don't know them all. A small hotel in Middlesbrough. A bingo hall in Hartlepool. Some shops. A pub. Maybe an industrial factory near Middlesbrough. Such things. Many such things.'

'Quite a portfolio,' I mused. 'A lot of interests,' I added.

I wondered what the Slovaks were particularly interested in. Businesses that turned cash over, obviously, if they were money

176

laundering. Outlets for drugs, too. But industrial plants could also be useful, depending on what they were set up to do. Then again, property was good if you wanted to invest for the future. Perhaps they were in for the long haul.

'Did Harry have any overseas interests?'

'No. Only the villa in Rhodes.'

'Holiday home?'

'Yes.'

'Whereabouts?'

'I don't know. How long do you think it will be before they contact me, Frank?'

My turn to shrug. 'Depends how fast they can get lawyers on the case. Days, like I said, if they've done their homework. Weeks otherwise. I don't know.'

She could be stuck here for a while, in the wind and the isolation. I wondered how long she would stick it out.

'Did you go to the villa in Rhodes often?'

'Once only. Maybe twice. I don't know where it was.'

How likely was that? I wondered. But I didn't press. It seemed to be a subject she had little interest in discussing.

'The guy that contacted you last night? Was he the boss?'

'Yes.'

'Does he have a name?'

'Sandor.'

'Sandor?'

'You are right,' she said, anticipating my next question. 'It is not a Slovak name. It is Hungarian.'

She was ahead of me. I hadn't been questioning the guy's ethnicity. I just hadn't heard her properly.

'That what he is — Hungarian?'

'Yes.' She frowned with thought. 'How do you say? He is Hungarian, by his family and culture, but he is Slovak citizen. He is born in Slovakia, and belongs there.'

'Sounds complicated.'

'There are many such people. Czechs, too. Not only Slovaks live in Slovakia, but all are Slovaks by law. Do you understand?'

'Something to do with being born the wrong side of a new border?'

'Yes, exactly. Our countries are complicated. It is not like this one. You have the sea to say where your border is.'

I nodded towards the cliff edge and said, 'But the sea keeps changing it.'

She smiled. She seemed more relaxed. I had diverted her. But I was still pondering the villa in Rhodes, the existence of which she had inadvertently disclosed.

★   ★   ★

178

Jimmy Mack knew something was going on. Obviously he did. For a brief moment he had been on the frontline of the action, and he knew it wasn't over. But he didn't quiz me. He knew everything would come out eventually, and he knew that with the game in progress I wouldn't want to do too much explaining at present. He didn't mind. He never did. He was a patient man. Besides, I believe he enjoyed the intrigue and occasional excitement my activities brought into his life. There was only so much satisfaction you could get out of mending lobster pots all day long.

So, later, Jimmy was quite happy to entertain a beautiful young woman while I caught up on one or two things I had been neglecting.

I started in my cottage. It didn't take me long to go through Vlasta's meagre collection of possessions. As expected, I didn't find what I wanted there. So I gave Jimmy and Vlasta a wave and set off for the big house in the hills.

★   ★   ★

There were no cars parked there. Nothing about the outside of the house looked any different. My guess was that no one had been there since my visit with Vlasta.

I collected the key from its hiding place and let myself into the house. I shut the door after me. Then I stood for a moment, listening and scenting. The house smelled even more lifeless. Not stale, not yet, but empty of human occupants. It seemed a pity. I liked the house. I liked everything about it, apart from the last owner.

I didn't bother with the downstairs. What I wanted wouldn't be there. I headed straight for the bedrooms. What was obviously the master bedroom was huge. It had two separate full-width windows, and a bathroom adjacent. The décor was opulent Greek, from about two thousand years ago. Lots of marble and urns and busts. Stuff like that.

One wall was all wardrobe. I opened the doors. So far as I could see, there was nothing of a masculine nature in there. There was no space for it. Vlasta had a lot of clothes.

I went quickly through the racks, finding nothing of interest. I didn't find what I wanted in the overhead lockers either. Just empty bags and cases.

Harry's wardrobe, in another room, took more time. He had about thirty suits, all of them with pockets galore. Then there was the rack of shirts, many with breast pockets. Again, though, I found nothing relevant. I was fast running out of easy options. Next, I was going to have to go through books and papers.

There were bound to be some. I didn't believe everything would be kept in office filing cabinets. There would have been times when Harry wanted stuff close at hand, so he could deal with it out of office hours.

Probably he had a study or an office here, possibly downstairs. First, though, the open door of another bedroom made me pause. I considered it and then stepped inside and looked around. Hannah's room, obviously. Girly stuff on the walls. I opened a wardrobe and saw she had almost as many clothes as her mother. I sighed. Was it worth bothering?

I started searching and found what I wanted very quickly. Hannah kept scrapbooks. I smiled when I saw the first one. What an old-fashioned idea! Somehow it didn't fit with modern children's lives. I picked the first one up and scanned through it. Celebs. Celebs in extraordinary variety.

Footballers and film stars. Singers and dancers. And people she probably had just liked the look of.

The second scrapbook was Hannah's 'Nature Trove'. Pictures, photos, poems, bits of Hannah-composed and handwritten text. It seemed very Hannah-ish. I smiled again, remembering how she had been with me.

Then I put it down. I was intruding.

The next book was pure gold, a true treasure chest. It contained photos, pictures and information concerning the holiday travels of Hannah and her family. Zoo entrance tickets. Museum stickers. Maps. Restaurant receipts. Everything in geographical order, the English, the Scottish, the Czech, the Slovak and the Greek. The last section contained, amongst much else, a receipt for a television that had been delivered to an address in Pefkos, Rhodes.

Thank you, Hannah. My search was over. I tucked that scrapbook under my arm and left.

24

Vlasta and I wandered down to the beach. Early evening. The tide was rising. Stiff breeze. Cool air on the face. Vlasta took hold of my hand. She laughed with mock terror as she slipped and might have fallen over the edge, had I not held her tight.

She seemed to like that, the holding tight. She moved close and gripped me hard. She raised her face, eyes like slits and her lips beckoned. I stooped and kissed her. She kissed back, hard. I could feel her beneath the thin shirt that was all she wore. The fabric moved across her skin. She moaned and rubbed against me. I could feel her nipples, hard and big. I cupped one hand around her breast. She liked that. She liked me.

But I didn't trust her.

We broke apart and stared at each other.

'Later,' she said. 'Yes?'

'Yes.'

I wanted her, and she knew it, but I didn't trust her. Things were not as she had said.

* * *

We walked along the beach a little way. Not far. The tide was still some way off the high water mark but when it came in there would be no sand left. The sea would be up hard against the base of the cliffs. There would be no escape for anyone foolish enough still to be here.

We returned to the bottom of the rough track down the cliff face and sat on rocks to watch the sea do its job. Spray flew in sheets through the air, carried by a breeze that sailors would have loved. There was white water before us, and beyond that line after line of breakers.

'It is beautiful here,' Vlasta said, nuzzling against me.

I laughed. 'That's not what you said the first time you came to Risky Point.'

'I was young then,' she said with a shy smile. 'I didn't know any better.'

I laughed again. This Vlasta was wonderful. There was nowhere I would rather have been at that moment, but I knew it couldn't last. And I was damned certain she did, too.

'The children would like it here,' she said reflectively. 'They love the sea.'

Tricky ground, this. I knew I had to skirt it carefully. 'It's a bit cold and dangerous,' I suggested.

'Oh, yes! But they would love it.'

'They wouldn't be able to swim here.'

'No, but there are other things. Even just to see it.'

'I agree,' I said with a smile. 'That's what keeps me here against all reason. One of these days, one of these years, or hopefully centuries, the sea will probably take my cottage. Until then, I will stay.'

'Yes, you should. It suits you here, I think.'

We were silent for a while. Then I said, 'But sometimes it would be nice to be somewhere where the sea is warm and calm, and you can swim all day if you want to.'

'Oh, yes. Hannah and Petr love swimming, too. They often . . . Holidays . . . ,' she added vaguely with a shrug.

I wondered what she had nearly said before she had managed to stop herself. My guess was that it would have been something about Rhodes, the villa by the warm Mediterranean or Aegean, and the blistering white sand. My growing belief was that that was where Hannah and Petr were, along with Harry. Soon, perhaps, Vlasta would join them there.

Why else would she tell me so little about it? Her big mistake had been to mention the villa in Rhodes in the first place. I was sure no one else knew about it.

★ ★ ★

All that evening the thoughts simmered in my head. Vlasta was a fine actress. There was no doubt about it. A good makeup artist, too. When she had turned up on my doorstep for the second time, a beaten wife, she had convinced me. From that moment on I had not doubted anything she had said. Now I doubted everything.

A big question was why she had ever involved me in the first place. Or why *they* had come to my door. Perhaps they had been looking for a mug to give their intended disappearance credibility?

What was it, she had said of me? A good man, but poor. Something like that. Exactly the kind they needed. Someone eager to earn a bit of money by performing a simple job well. I hadn't been only a driver. I had also been a witness to Harry's appalling behaviour, and someone who could testify to Vlasta's desperate flight away from him. The ten grand had been a cheap investment for them.

Bill Peart had given me the basis for their story right at the beginning. Harry was in trouble, financially. He knew there was no easy way out for him. Rather than lose everything, he had decided to bale out now with whatever cash he could liquidate.

Much, if not all the cash no doubt

186

belonged to his new partner, Sandor. Perhaps Harry had figured that for a time, at least, Sandor would be content just to take over the whole business — it was what he had wanted — leaving Harry to run to his secret bolthole with the cash he had salvaged and everything else dear to him, namely Vlasta and the kids. All that was left now was for Vlasta to slip away and join him. End of story.

There were one or two awkward bits in this construction but they weren't too hard to surmount once the basic structure was in place. Vlasta's parents, for example. Well, my guess was that they weren't that at all. Her parents, that is. Perhaps they were simply collaborators who had reached the end of their useful lives, and knew too much to be left alone in retirement. Vlasta's distress had been as well faked as so much else since she had come into my life.

The Slovaks, of course, had got wind of Harry's intentions. It had probably been them who had pursued us and the money bag so relentlessly across Belgium and Germany. It hadn't mattered to them who was in the Toyota, or what happened to them, so long as they salvaged the cash.

Things fitted so well now. I had the picture.

I still wasn't sure who had lifted the kids from the guest house in Jetřichovice, but that was a detail. Initially, I had assumed it had been the Slovaks; now I believed it had been Harry. Vlasta had acted the part of the distraught mother exceedingly well.

So there we were. I felt, if not happier, certainly more sure of my ground at last. And I knew what I was going to do next. Without any doubt at all, I knew where I was going next, too.

25

It was a four-hour flight from Manchester. Most of the way I was happy to rest with my eyes closed. The last few days had been tough. I needed the rest.

I had only hand luggage and was soon out of the terminal at the other end. Middle of the day. The heat and the light hit me hard. It was blistering. The white concrete showed no mercy. Even the wind was scorching. The sea was blue, of course, quite unlike the one I knew so well at Risky Point. No doubt it was warmer, too.

I hired a VW Golf and was out of the airport precinct in short order. My fellow passengers were still waiting with trepidation around the luggage carousel.

I had seen a very generalized map and knew Pefkos was at the opposite, western end of the island, just beyond Lindos. Not far, maybe twenty miles away. And I had time to spare. So a little way down the road I swung into a small shopping development and parked outside a café. Time to relax and think through my next move properly. Time, as well, to study the more detailed map that had come with the car.

★ ★ ★

Vlasta wouldn't be here yet. She couldn't possibly be. She didn't know where I was either. I had told her I had other business to attend to, things that couldn't wait. I would be away a couple of days. My guess was that she would have given me time to get clear and then would have made her way to an airport, perhaps calling in at the old house to collect anything else she didn't want to abandon.

She might have left me a note, saying, for example: Thank you, Frank, for everything you have done. Now I must move on alone and search for my children. Good-bye, Frank. Something like that. Then she would aim to drop off the map.

I could see it. I knew exactly how her scheming, conniving little mind worked now. So I wanted to be there, in Pefkos, for the big reunion. I wanted to see her tears of joy as she caught up with Harry and he welcomed her back to what now was to be their permanent home.

Hannah and Petr would just take it all in their stride, of course. They were young enough. Their new life in a home they already knew, by a warm sea, would be an exciting prospect. And I wouldn't take any of it away from them. I just wanted Vlasta and Harry to know they hadn't fooled me, and for them to feel guilty about what they had done. As if they would — either of them!

★   ★   ★

No hurry. So I took my time and drifted down the island, missing out the delights of Faliraki, spending a couple of hours in much more delightful Lindos and finally making Pefkos as the sun was going down.

Lindos was an old fishing village that had become a tourist attraction without losing its character and style. Compact, tightly packed, with narrow alleys threading their way through the medieval structure of the village, it was everything that Pefkos was not. Pefkos was new, modern, spread out and a creation for tourists. It was pleasant enough. Bars and restaurants, and small hotels and apartment blocks bordered the sea; palm trees and bougainvillea in full bloom decorated the area, and stood in marked contrast to the harsh, dry hills immediately behind the village.

Either side of the road there were occasional new houses, villas in white, often with shade trees that must have been planted already fully grown. I drove slowly along the road until I reached the current end of Pefkos. Then I turned back and looked for a place to stay for a night or two. It wasn't difficult. The season was not yet in full swing, and the Greek economy was in . . . well, confusion.

I took a room in a small hotel with a balcony looking out to sea and its own pool. Then I had a meal in the little restaurant and decided to do nothing more until daylight returned. I wanted to give Vlasta time to get here.

★ ★ ★

The next morning it was easy enough to find the address Hannah had so carefully saved. The house was set at the foot of a hillside strewn with outcrops of limestone, occasional palm trees and patches of dense evergreen shrubs. It was an architect's house, all glass and white concrete, albeit with a red pantiled roof. It was a house built for someone who didn't care much for neighbours, and wanted them kept at a distance, someone who valued privacy or had things to hide. Perfect for Vlasta and Harry.

I whiled away the hours. From the car and from one or two small cafés and bars I had distant views of Harry's house and the drive leading up to it. I saw no cars or people entering or leaving the property. Admittedly, they could have sneaked in or out when I wasn't looking, but I grew impatient. I needed to satisfy myself that Vlasta really hadn't arrived yet. The best way of doing that was getting up close and having a look.

When the sun dipped towards the horizon and shadows were lengthening all around, I made my move. I headed for the house I had been watching all day.

I had seen a man herding his goats through the scrub below the house, moving parallel to the road but a couple of hundred yards inland. That suggested a track. I went looking for it, and found it. Nothing much. Not tarmac or even a proper stone path. More just a way through the wilderness, a trod that allowed you to avoid the cactus spines and the ferocious needles of the strange bushes that eked out a living on that rocky, desert landscape.

I followed the track until it intersected the drive leading to the gates fronting the house. Then I abandoned caution and walked up the drive. To hell with it! I was tiring of this game I was playing. I wanted to get on with it, and then get out of there. The novelty and challenge were wearing off. This land was too hot and too dry for me. And I was sick of

Harry's little world. Vlasta's too.

The black iron gates were high and wide, with a gilt arrow head at the top of each of the many shafts. They were closed, and no doubt locked. They would purr open electronically at the approach of a welcome visitor, just like the gates I'd seen in B&Q. But they stayed resolutely shut for me.

I moved to the side and followed the boundary wall until I found a place where the razor wire had run out and I could climb over. Surprisingly, perhaps, I had seen no CCTV cameras, or anything else elaborate in the way of security. Harry must have felt secrecy was protection enough.

The light was going fast now. I could see my way clearly enough as I moved across the ground beneath the whispering palms, but in another hour it would be difficult. There were lights on in the house. Several rooms were lit. I smiled with satisfaction. I was looking forward to surprising the Georges — all of them.

I skirted round the house, staying well back but close enough to see inside. The kitchen was empty, illuminated but empty. So, too, was a living room. Other rooms were dark. The final room on the ground floor was lit but closed blinds meant I could see nothing. After that I was back at the front door.

I hesitated. To ring the bell, or not? I decided not.

The door was unlocked. I opened it and stepped inside. There I paused, listening out for the kind of sounds that people like Hannah and Petr tend to make — kids' noise. Nothing. They were either out or busy with a computer game or something. I smiled and moved on.

Nobody was in any of the downstairs rooms. I tried them all and drew blanks all the way round. By then, I wasn't feeling so good about this. The family wasn't in residence. But would they have gone out leaving the front door unlocked? Was Rhodes really that crime free?

I paused in the hallway, at the foot of the wide flight of marble stairs. Nymphs and gods and things studied me intently from their alcoves in the curving wall. Still, I could hear nothing. No sounds from either upstairs or down. I shrugged and set off up the stairs.

The door to a room on the first floor was open. Light spilled out onto the marble floor ahead of me. I shrugged and made for the open door. Now I was here, I might as well have a look round, even if the place was, for the moment, unoccupied.

He was waiting for me.

A colossal hit in the back sent me sprawling

into the room. I slid face-down across the polished floor, breathless and in agony. It felt like my back was broken.

Later, I worked out that he must have been standing on a narrow stone shelf above the doorway, a shelf that ran around the room and normally supported ornaments. But at the time I had no idea where the attack had come from.

As my momentum slowed, I scrabbled sideways desperately but he was too quick for me and delivered a kick to the head that shut off my brain.

When I came round, it was to find myself sitting on the floor, arms stretched and tied behind me very tightly. My head was sunk onto my chest. I raised it slightly and tried to clear my vision. Then I wished I was still unconscious — or had never entered the room, or the house, in the first place.

Leroy stepped forward and kicked me again in the head. I was in agony, as well as in shock. I dropped my head back down, trying to protect my jaw.

'Who came with you?' he said.

'What?'

'I haven't time for this,' he said, kicking me in the ribs, making me cry out with pain. 'Who came with you? Where are they?'

Dimly, I perceived the reason why I wasn't

already dead. Leroy wanted information.

'Kick me again,' I muttered, 'and you risk never knowing — until it's too late.'

I wanted badly to know where Harry and Vlasta were but instinct told me to give nothing away by asking questions. I wanted to survive. Very badly I wanted that, even if my chances seemed almost non-existent.

Leroy was on edge. As my senses began to clear, I wondered why. He was like a coiled spring. Gone was the relaxed demeanour of the killer I'd seen at work in Dêĉín.

'The Slovaks bring you?'

'Yeah.'

'The lying bastards!'

I clutched onto the straw he'd handed me. It wasn't much but there was nothing else I could reach.

'Special plane,' I said.

'How many? How many men?' he repeated when I didn't answer.

I shook my head. 'I didn't see them all.'

'Three or four, or more?'

'More, I think.'

He started pacing. I could tell he was thinking. He was in a bind. Wasn't sure what to do to get out of it.

'How did you know about this place?' he demanded, whirling on me again. 'She tell you?'

I guessed he meant Vlasta. I nodded. His question confused me but I nodded anyway.

'Where are they now?'

I shook my head. I meant it as a gesture to deny knowledge. He took it as a sign of non-compliance. The knife appeared in his hand. It clicked open. I could guess the way it would go now. Bit by bit, he intended cutting information out of me. First, the ears, probably, then the nose, and the eyes, until I begged him to finish it.

'What about the money?' I blurted out with desperate inspiration.

'I've got it.'

'Not that! The money that was here already.'

He smiled that dreadful smile of his. 'Harry never mentioned any other money What are you on about?'

So Harry wasn't here. Nor, perhaps, was Vlasta. And I'd not heard the children. Suddenly, the pieces in the puzzle rearranged themselves and clicked into a new pattern. I'd got it wrong, I realized. Very wrong.

'That's why they're coming,' I said hoarsely, my voice fading to a faint croak. 'For the money!'

I started coughing and whispered, 'Water! Please.'

He was eager to hear more, and I was

desperate to tell him, but I was coughing and choking. My voice had dried up.

I heard the kitchen tap being turned on. Water splashed into the sink. A glass or cup was filled. I didn't look up, my head down on my chest. He came back. I knew he would need both hands to get liquid into me.

Through slits in my half-closed eyes, I saw him lean down and reach forward with a glass. The knife was not in either hand now.

It was a high-risk manoeuvre but there were no safe options for me now. With a sudden convulsion, I arced my lower body and swung my right leg upwards to kick him in the balls. I kicked as hard as I've ever kicked anything, and got it right. He yelped and dropped the glass. He stooped forward, holding his groin, and I kicked him in the face with full power. He tried to step back, but I twisted, caught his legs with mine and brought him down, flat on his back.

There was no time. It was a mad, desperate struggle. I knew the knife would soon be in his hand again. I did what I could, what I had to do.

I cracked my boot heel down into his face, and felt bone smash. I raised my leg and drove the heel down again, and again. I kept on doing the same thing until I could no longer lift my leg any more. Then I did the same thing with my other leg. I did it until I knew it was no longer necessary. I did it until his face had smashed and spread into a mish-mash of bone, gristle and skin.

When I stopped I curled sideways and fought to get air into my lungs. The pressure eased. My heart rate began to slow. I turned on to my back again. My vision began to clear now the frenzy was over, and the sight of my own feet awash with blood made me vomit. I bent my knees and raised my legs to kick Leroy's body away from me.

Somehow I got up. First to my knees, and then to my feet. I took my time and avoided looking at or thinking about anything that wasn't absolutely essential to the task of standing upright. That accomplished, my focus was on getting my hands free. Until I did that I wouldn't be able to think, and there was an awful lot to think about. More than ever.

26

I found the kitchen, ignoring the footprints I was leaving on the snowy white marble of the staircase and floors. A block of chef's knives caught my eye. I sat up on the counter and managed to work a knife out of the block. The best I could do then was jam it, by the handle, into a drawer and start to saw at whatever was binding my wrists. My fear was that I would get the positioning of the knife wrong, or it would slip, and I would find myself leaking blood from a major artery.

So I did it slowly and carefully, hoping no one else arrived in the house before it was done. It took an age, and much frustration, but eventually the binding was sufficiently parted for me to be able to snap the remaining strands. It was nylon cord, I saw then. Lucky for me Leroy hadn't used plastic cable ties. They would have been beyond my capabilities.

I massaged my wrists. Then I looked down and almost vomited again when I saw my feet. Fucking Leroy! His face and brains were all over me. I put my feet in the sink and turned on the tap. Eventually, most of the blood had run off. My lower legs were soaked, my boots were full of water, but I was clean.

I took my boots off and emptied them. I squeezed my trousers out, and the boots went back on my feet. That done, I still had to do something about the mess upstairs. First, though, I went through the house, searching for clues and information about what had been going on here.

It looked as though Leroy hadn't been here long. The signs, the evidence, were everywhere. Hardly anything was out of place. He had arrived, probably at night, and flopped onto a bed and gone to sleep. His bag was still packed. Beside it, amazingly, was something with which I was familiar: the money bag Vlasta had brought into my life. The money, or most of it, was still inside.

I shook my head wearily and suppressed a sigh. Vlasta, how I misjudged you!

*   *   *

I rang Bill Peart.

'Where the hell are you?' he asked suspiciously. He must have been looking at the strange server names appearing on his screen.

'I admit it,' I told him. 'I'm far away.'

'Greece?'

'Yeah.'

'So the job is finished? You're on your hols?'

'If only! I'll tell you about it later. For now, can you tell me anything more about Harry George? It's important, Bill.'

'The dead guy? It's important?'

'Is it him, Bill? Is he really dead?'

'Without a doubt.'

'It couldn't be a case of mistaken identity?'

'No chance. One of our guys went out to take a look. In addition we got DNA. It was Harry.'

'Thanks, Bill.'

I switched off before he could question me further. He would be frustrated, annoyed even, but I would sort it out with him later. Hell, I might even close his case for him.

So, apologies, Harry — as well as Vlasta. I misjudged you both. I misjudged you all, in fact, Leroy included.

It all looked so very different now. It looked now as if Leroy really had taken out Harry. I wondered if he'd had the mysterious Sandor's blessing or had just gone into business for himself. Hard to say.

In any case, he hadn't had Sandor's approval to take the cash bag. That was why he had been so worried. My arrival hadn't frightened him, but thought of Sandor close behind had. He must be some guy, this Sandor.

Clearly, Leroy had over-extended himself. He had been unable to resist the temptation when it appeared before him. Harry was down, finished, and the money bag was there with him, begging to be picked up. Leroy had realized he had the perfect place to go with it, as well. Harry's little hidey hole, which nobody else knew about. Except Vlasta. But he would have figured he could handle her if she ever showed up. He would enjoy doing it, too.

Then I had appeared, and made him fearful the Slovaks were on their way. They still wanted their money back, and now they knew where he had gone with it. It was too much. The great plan had unravelled.

The Slovaks might well have persuaded Leroy to change his allegiance and help them by doing away with Harry, but I thought it more likely that Leroy had been working for himself. Perhaps he'd had it with Harry, anyway. He'd seen the writing on the wall. The good times were over, the business going down the tubes, new owners set to take over. Leroy's best option had been to take out Harry, grab the cash and disappear. So he'd taken it.

Then I'd turned up, hot on his trail. He'd been paranoid. And he'd got careless. And I'd got lucky.

* * *

There was nothing for me in Pefkos now. I bundled Leroy up in a rug and dragged him out into the wild land, where I scratched and dug a hole and buried him as deep as I could. By then, it was getting light again and I was pretty well knackered, but I did the best I could to wash the place down with a mop and a swill of hot water.

After that I checked through the villa again but found nothing more of interest. The place was just an empty house.

Finally, I looked at the cash bag and knew I couldn't risk taking it with me. Not that much money. A million quid? Christ! If I got stopped at the airport, and it got opened, I could face years of investigation and a real possibility of being locked up after years of legal proceedings. It wasn't worth it.

So I compromised. I opened the bag and took out twenty grand, ten for me and ten for Vlasta. It was an amount I reckoned I could reasonably say I'd won in a casino, if I did get stopped. Then I wrapped the bag in plastic sheeting and buried it in the garden directly underneath a sundial mounted on the wall.

That done, I drove back to the airport, dropped off the hire car and caught a flight to Manchester. Some hapless holiday-maker had not turned up or had taken ill, creating a last-minute opening for me to get out of there.

★   ★   ★

Manchester was predictably cold and damp. If cricket was being played at Old Trafford, it would be by players swathed in umpteen sweaters. Even footballers would be wearing gloves. To me, though, it felt good.

Even better was the cool wind at Risky Point. It was so invigorating. I didn't miss the heat of Rhodes at all.

Vlasta was out of sorts. She was laid on her bed, neither sleeping nor reading. Sulking, it looked like.

'Where have you been?' she demanded.

'I told you. I had business to attend to.'

She turned her face to the wall. I took pity on her. She must be going crazy thinking about the children.

'Come down and have a coffee with me, or a beer. Tell me what's been happening.'

She raised herself. 'You must be hungry,' she said. 'I will make some lunch.'

I was hungry, actually. I hadn't been thinking about it, but I was, I realized. Vlasta followed me downstairs and I let her have her way in the kitchen. Distraction therapy. More of it.

I wanted to talk about some of the stuff going round in my head, but not immediately. I needed to work my way to it gently, instead of blundering in and giving Vlasta hysterics.

We sat down to a meal of cold meats, cheese, fresh bread, fruit, and sundry bits and pieces, some of which I didn't even recognize let alone know I'd had in the house.

'I did some shopping while you were away,' Vlasta said, in response to my query. 'Jimmy took me in his truck.'

'That old thing? I'm surprised it reached the shops.'

She shrugged, unmollified. Her face was set to glum. I thought I knew why, so I didn't ask. But I was wrong.

'You don't trust me,' she said, giving me a disappointed look.

'What on earth makes you say that?'

'You don't trust me.'

'Of course I do!'

I had to say that, even though she was right. I wondered what had brought this on.

'You didn't do what you said you would do.'

I struggled to make sense of that. 'When?' I asked.

'You went to Rhodes. You didn't tell me.'

That shook me. I was caught flat-footed.

'Is it the suntan that makes you think that?' I asked, peering hard at my forearms. 'It must be.'

She tossed her head with annoyance. 'You went to the villa?' she asked.

There was no way out or round it now. Jokes wouldn't do it. And she seemed quite certain about where I'd been. She wasn't just guessing.

'What do you know?' I asked.

'Your friend came here, your policeman friend. He told me. So it's no use lying to me.'

Bill Peart. I winced. I hadn't thought of that possibility, being given away by him.

'Bill doesn't know what I've been doing the past few days.'

'Maybe not, but I do. He wanted to know when you would be back from Rhodes. That was enough for me.'

'What did you tell him?'

'Nothing. I said I knew nothing. He seemed angry.'

He would have been. I had some explaining to do.

'Vlasta, you're right. I didn't trust you. I

don't trust any of my clients. They lie to me, they distort the truth, they fail to tell me things that are important, and sometimes they put my life as well as theirs in danger. So until I know them better, I can't afford to trust them.'

'I thought we knew each other very well,' she said bitterly. 'I slept with you!'

Dear God! She would be saying she thought I loved her next.

'Vlasta, you only told me some things. You didn't tell me everything I needed to know.'

'Like what?'

'Like nearly everything! First, you wouldn't tell me where we were going. Then . . . Too many things to list. Where the money came from, who Harry's new business partner was. Finally, you pretended you didn't know anything about Harry's villa in Rhodes — you had only been there once or twice, you said — when it was obvious to me that you must have been there many times. You knew exactly where it was.'

'I had my reasons,' she said, tossing her head.

'I'm sure you did. But so did I for not trusting you. I got to thinking, what if Harry isn't really dead at all? What if the money you were carrying was to be the basis of a new life together with him and the children? What if you were all going to meet up again in the secret villa, that nobody else knew about, in Rhodes?'

'Harry is dead,' she said sullenly. 'The policeman said it was true.'

'I know that now, but I didn't then.'

She dumped the celery stick she had been gnawing down on her plate and pushed the plate away. 'It is true,' she said. 'I didn't tell you everything. But you were only partly correct.'

'Oh?'

'I didn't tell you about the villa because I intended going there with the children, and I wanted no one else to know anything about it. I did want us to have a new life together, me and the children.'

'Without Harry?'

'Yes! Without him. Everything I said was true. I hated him. I told you the truth about him.'

That much, at least, I could believe now.

'Now,' she added, 'my dream is ruined. Harry is dead. But the money is gone also. And my children are gone. You know about the villa. Everything is finished!'

Maybe it wasn't, but I didn't say so for the moment. I watched as she poured us both some coffee.

'Did you find the villa?' she asked when she

had calmed down.

I nodded. 'It was easy to find.'

I didn't tell her that Hannah's magpie habits were what had made it easy. I didn't want to risk setting mother against daughter. But there was other stuff I did need to tell her.

'It seems someone else had thoughts similar to yours, Vlasta.'

'What do you mean?' She peered at me, puzzled.

'The house wasn't empty. I expected to find you and Harry and the children there. Instead, I found Leroy.'

'Leroy!'

Her shock was genuine. There was no doubt about that.

'I believe he murdered Harry and fled to Rhodes to start a new life. You weren't the only one with that idea.'

She shook her head vigorously. 'He wouldn't do that. Leroy was Harry's man. He did much terrible work for Harry.'

'Leroy was Leroy's man. In the end he probably got tired of Harry, and saw an opportunity to get out and go somewhere nobody else knew about.'

'Leroy knew about the villa?'

'He was there when I arrived.'

She shrugged. 'But he had no money. He

had only his wages.'

I shook my head. 'Wrong. Leroy had the bag they took from me in Jetřichovice. Leroy had it, and the money was all still there.'

Her eyes widened at that, as she began to realize the implications.

'You found him there, in the villa?'

I nodded and watched her begin calculating.

'Yet you are here. So where is Leroy now?'

I let her figure that out for herself.

'You are here, alive, Frank. So Leroy is . . . not alive? Is that it?'

I said nothing again. I saw no need to be more explicit, not even when she threw herself at me, apparently overjoyed.

She still hadn't told me everything. I wanted more from her.

27

'We still don't know where Hannah and Petr are,' I reminded her. 'They must be with the Slovaks, this Sandor guy.'

She sat up straight and pushed her hair back out of her face, reluctantly accepting that reality hadn't disappeared altogether.

'Don't you think it's time to tell me what you know about them?' I pressed. 'And it's no use telling me you know nothing. I'm not going to accept that.'

She got up and began to pace around the room. I lay back and watched her. I was in no hurry. I could wait. I could do patience.

'What do you want to know?' she said suddenly, wheeling on me.

'It's simple, Vlasta. I need to know who they are, what they do, how they got here, where they are from — everything. They have the children. We want the children back. I need information. OK?'

'You don't love me, do you?' she said sadly.

'Jesus Christ, Vlasta!'

'You don't. I can tell. You don't trust me. And you ask too many questions. You are not content with what I tell you.'

I lay back and stared at the ceiling. Of all the wacky women with whom I had whiled away a few hours, this one was becoming a stand-out classic.

'Look at me, Vlasta,' I said at last, sitting upright. 'I want to find Hannah and Petr, and I want to find them alive. It's as simple as that for me. They are my priority. Everything else — including you and me,' I added desperately, 'comes after that. Got it?'

She nodded. 'But it is not so simple,' she added.

No, I'd never thought it would be when Vlasta was involved. No surprises there. Now she sighed and made a big effort.

'Sandor contacted Harry. He wanted to do some business with him. I knew nothing at first, but that's how it was. Then Harry wanted me to meet Sandor and talk to him. So I did.

'After that, Harry said he would do business with Sandor. I don't know what they agreed. But I think Harry needed money. Maybe he borrowed some from Sandor. Then maybe they agreed that Sandor would have a share of the business, in exchange. Something like that, I think.

'That is all,' she concluded, staring hard at me, daring me to contradict her.

No, it wasn't all. But I just nodded. At least

it was a start. I didn't need to pull out her finger nails, one by one.

'There came a time,' I said carefully, 'when Harry had to pay Sandor back a lot of money, a lot of cash, and you saw an opportunity to grab it and get out. Leave them to sort it out between themselves. That how it was?'

'Yes. Exactly.'

I doubted that as well, but again I didn't say anything. 'So now we come to the big question. If Sandor has the kids, and is keeping them until you sign the papers transferring ownership to him of Harry's businesses, where are they?'

Vlasta shrugged.

It crossed my mind that she was remarkably cool about the whereabouts and fate of the children now. It was as if the shock waves from their abduction had subsided. She was getting used to the idea. At least Harry didn't have them. Maybe that was what she was thinking.

Tough kid, our Vlasta. Trained in the school of hard knocks. Well able to look after herself, and hers. I didn't like her so much now.

'So you don't know where they are?' I pressed. 'You have no idea?'

'Of course not.'

'Well, let's explore the possibilities. You said Sandor is from Bratislava, the capital.'

'He is now, yes. But not originally.'

'But that's where he's based?'

'Yes.'

It was like pulling teeth.

'He has property in Bratislava? Businesses?'

She shrugged. 'Probably. I don't know.'

I got up and moved across to the window. Something wasn't right here. But I didn't know what. I just couldn't put my finger on it. I still had only part of the picture. That was the trouble. And I had no idea what the rest of it looked like.

'The sea is rough,' Vlasta said, coming to stand next to me, pressing against me.

I nodded. I could feel the heat of her through the thin blouse she wore. I knew what I wanted to do. Somehow I held off. But, God, she must have been some exotic dancer. No wonder Harry had wanted her so badly for his club, and then for other things.

'Where was Sandor from originally?'

'A small town in Slovakia.'

'Called?'

'Zuberec. It is in the mountains, *Zápardné Tatry*, the Western Tatras.'

'What's it like?'

'It is very small. A village, only.'

She chuckled and moved away, resigned to having failed to distract me. 'It is terrible! There is nothing there, but it is in the mountains and some people like it for that reason. But, as everywhere in Slovakia, it is better now than it used to be. Some people have built new houses. But the old houses are horrible. Black, timber buildings with few windows.'

She shuddered, leaving me in no doubt about her feelings for Zuberec.

'You have been there?'

'Yes. A long time ago. It is one of the places in the Tatras where we Czechs and Slovaks would go with our families for holidays.' She gave another little shudder and added, 'Now I don't like mountains, and I don't like such places as Zuberec.'

That was plain enough. I could take a hint. She really didn't like it.

But I knew a hell of a lot more now, and an idea was growing.

'Sandor will have family there still?'

'In Zuberec?' She grimaced. 'I don't know. Maybe. Why?'

I shrugged. What I was thinking was it might be a good place to keep children hostage. Small children don't need gangsters to look after them. They need women. Mothers, grandmothers, sisters. Did Sandor have women like that he could call on?

Vlasta said maybe. It was possible. That was what I thought, too.

I was beginning to think I knew where I was going next.

'Have you heard from the Slovaks again, by the way?'

'Yes. It is the same thing. They say I must wait. They say lawyers will contact me when the documents are ready for signing. Until then I must do nothing. If I do that, the children will be safe.'

Maybe, I thought. That word again.

'Have you been able to speak to Hannah or Petr?'

She shook her head.

That worried me. Not Vlasta, though, seemingly. She was surprisingly trusting.

'Did they say anything about Leroy?'

'No, nothing.'

'Or Harry?'

'No.'

That was interesting. It meant they were not linking Leroy with Harry, or Vlasta now. It meant they considered Leroy to be their business. I felt even more certain that they had recruited the one to take care of the other, and that Leroy had exceeded his brief and done a runner when he saw the cash bag.

'We'll just have to wait,' I said.

She nodded.

I began to make plans.

28

I was anticipating meeting Sandor eventually in Zuberec, but I got to meet him sooner than that. I was talking to Jimmy Mack when a car came nosing along the track to our cottages. Jimmy stared at it. I turned and looked, too. It was a black Audi with tinted windows, a powerful beast more suited to the autobahn than our track.

'Another one,' Jimmy said mysteriously.

'Looks like it.'

I resumed our conversation about the kind of weather and sea that ling and turbot like, and don't like, around the rocks, but Jimmy's mind was no longer on it. Nor was mine. We were both waiting to see who was inside the Audi.

It stopped alongside us. The driver's door opened and a man got out. Aged about forty, he was short and stocky, with short dark hair and a round face. Another man got out on the passenger side. He was much the same in build and appearance. Both were dressed in blue jeans, T-shirts and leather jackets.

'You know a guy called Doy? Lives around here?' the driver asked, unsmiling, looking serious. He had a deep voice and an American accent.

'That's me.'

'Yeah?'

He looked me up and down.

Jimmy sensed the situation and said, 'I'll be getting back now. I know what to do.'

'Sure, Jimmy. I'll see you later.'

He set off. I knew that depending on how things worked out, he would be either loading the shotgun or speed-dialling Bill Peart. I was happy for him to use his own judgement.

The driver watched Jimmy go and then turned back to his own man. He nodded at him and the passenger got back inside the car. Now there was just the two of us. Interesting.

'Let's cut through the crap, Doy. I'm Sandor. You may have heard of me?'

Even more interesting. I nodded.

'You know what's going on?'

'Some of it.'

He smiled now, as if he was sure he'd got the right man. 'Harry's dead,' he said, as if it would be important news to me.

'So I heard.'

'Yeah, well. Leroy. You know Leroy? Harry's right-hand man?'

'I met him a couple of times, once with your people in Dêčín.'

'That right?' He thought about it and nodded. 'Yeah. They told me. He went too far, Leroy.'

I waited with all the patience I could summon. He had things to say but I couldn't guess what they were.

'Leroy was supposed to be working for me.' He shook his head, as if it were a matter of big regret. 'He wasted Harry. You know that, too?'

'I guessed. It sounded like his handiwork.'

'He sure is handy with that knife of his. Leroy, eh? What a guy!' He spat into the dust and then grinned at me. 'Friend of yours?'

I met his gaze and shook my head. 'What do you think?'

'Me? I don't know. So I'm asking.'

There was something odd about this. Then it struck me: he didn't know! He was fishing. He hadn't come here to threaten or warn. He'd come to find out things that puzzled him.

'I told you. I met him. That's all. I hope you're going to tell me he's dead, as well as Harry?'

Sandor spun round and for a moment stared into the sky with frustration. He had energy to burn. He was doing his best to control it, but inside he was a volcano. He pulsed raw power in a way that Harry George had not. No games, I decided. No verbal jousting. I would be straightforward and aim to keep him at arm's length.

'OK,' he said now. 'Here's what I came for. You know where Leroy is?'

I shook my head.

'He took off — maybe with money doesn't belong to him. Where's he gone?'

'He was working for you, not me. How do you expect me to know? That bastard tried to kill us all, tried to run us off the autobahn — kids and their mother, as well as me.'

'I heard. Like I said, he went too far, got out of control.'

Almost a hint of sympathy and apology? I could almost believe that.

'Any ideas where he is now?'

'I haven't even thought about it. But no, I don't.'

'How about Vlasta? You thought about her?'

I stared at him and said, 'What's she got to do with it? She knows no more than me. What do you want, Sandor?'

He grinned. 'I want Leroy, and I want the money. Vlasta knows that. She also knows what else I want. Talk to her. Tell her.'

I stayed calm, determined not to over-react. 'If I see Leroy, I'll let you know. Give me a number where I can reach you.'

'Harry's club in Redcar,' he said. '*Aphrodite's*. Try there.'

He nodded for emphasis. Then he turned and got back in the car. He started the engine and turned the car round. Gave me a last look before setting off back down the track, taking it nice and easy. Cool and in control. Sandor. Nothing like Harry.

I looked over towards Jimmy's place and raised a hand to hold him off. No need for any more excitement.

★　★　★

'What did he want?' Vlasta asked.

'Leroy. And the money.'

'Does he know I am here?'

'I don't think so. You're just on the end of a phone at present. Better to keep it that way. He knows you'll have to turn up at the solicitor's office when the papers are ready.'

'Why is Sandor here himself?'

'He's come to take charge of his new business empire. He'll be keen to let the staff know he's the new Harry.'

She nodded. She looked terribly serious. I took pity on her. No point teasing. None at all.

'Do you trust him?' I asked.

'Trust him?'

'About the children.'

'I think he will return them when I do what he wants.'

'He might not.'

She shook her head vigorously. 'No. He will do that. I know him.'

No point telling her what I proposed to do, in that case.

29

I flew from Newcastle to Bratislava with Easyjet, who were the only airline going from a northern airport in the next few hours that still had spare seats. Vlasta didn't know about this, but I knew she might well work out where I'd gone before too long. It didn't matter. Some things I was better doing myself. This was one of them.

I hired a car at the airport, studied the road map that came with it and headed out into the Slovak interior, uncertain what I was going to find.

It took a couple of hours to get to Zuberec, most of the way on excellent roads. Most of the way, too, I could see the mountains. They were big ones, the Tatras, with jagged peaks that thrust into an azure sky dotted with small, white cumulus.

Zuberec was a farming village in the Western Tatras, as Vlasta had told me. On the way in I passed big fields being worked in almost medieval fashion, small groups of people cultivating individual strips of land. Most of the workers were women. From what I could see, potatoes were a big crop in this part of the world.

Again as Vlasta had said, the village was a mixture of new, concrete houses and old, black timber houses that looked as if they had been in place for centuries. There was a Roman Catholic church. I spotted a couple of small convenience stores and one or two restaurants or bars. Nothing else. It was a very impoverished looking place. Its saving grace was the nearby ring of mountains, with dark conifers cloaking the lower slopes and snow crusting the peaks. It looked like the kind of village to which people came in winter for simple skiing and in summer for simple walking. At no time of year would people come for fun or riotous entertainment.

There was plenty of accommodation available, *zimmer frei* or *pension*, which mostly amounted to rooms or apartments in someone's house. I paid for a couple of nights in advance in a pleasant little house tucked away in a back lane, but one night was probably more than I would need in Zuberec.

Already I was thinking I had made a mistake. Coming here looked like a waste of time and money. Whatever Vlasta had said, I couldn't link Sandor with his American accent to this village. Nor, for different reasons, could I place Hannah and Petr here.

For one thing, they would stand out like the proverbial sore thumb. Everyone would know they were here, and who they were. You can't keep secrets in a village like Zuberec.

But I had to look around and satisfy myself before I left, and I wouldn't be able to get home in one day anyway. There was nothing wrong with spending a night here, so I booked in and chatted for a while with the landlord in a mixture of languages. He was a genial fellow and he poured us both a glass of something like vodka to celebrate my arrival. It came out of an unmarked bottle and I guessed it was home-made. It was powerful stuff.

After that, I set off to perambulate around the village and get my bearings. I took no trouble to hide or disguise myself. The simple streets were back lanes between the houses, and they were pretty well empty. It looked like afternoons were a time to be home resting or gardening, which made me wonder what time people got up in the morning and started their work.

I wandered the sleepy streets with growing disenchantment, the energy and sense of purpose draining out of me by the minute. Vlasta would laugh with scorn when, and if, I told her where I'd been this time. Jimmy would shake his head and wonder where in the world I'd been. Bill Peart would be annoyed, as he so often was with me. And all of them would be fully justified. I was wasting my time. And I wasn't even enjoying myself.

It was hot. God, it was hot! I couldn't imagine what it would be like in July, when the sun really got to work. Dusty, too. And my ears were ringing with the hum of millions of insects. After a few minutes I decided it was no mystery why the locals packed in work at noon. Only a fool would be wandering around in this heat.

To ease their day, many of the locals had put small, plastic swimming pools in their gardens. Not much good if you were an Olympic hopeful, but perfect if you were a hot little kid and school had finished for the day. Or even if you were just someone who wanted to lie still in cool water. A belly flop in one sent a sheet of shining water skywards. I smiled and kept going, thinking I wouldn't mind a bit of that myself.

Naturally enough, the newer houses were mostly on the edges of the village. There, people with money, youth or energy had decided they had had enough of living in the traditional black timber houses and built themselves white concrete walls and red pantiled roofs. The gardens were little bigger, though. People still had to conserve their energies for the fields.

As I walked past one of the new houses, I glanced round when I heard a child shouting exuberantly at another. A girl was urging a younger boy to jump from the branch of a tree into a plastic pool. I paused and watched. The boy jumped. The resultant splash reached the top of the tree.

I could hardly believe my eyes. I walked on, my pulse racing. There was no doubt about it. I had just seen Hannah and Petr.

* * *

What to do now?

I kept going. I didn't look back.

At the end of the lane I paused and gazed out across a potato field. My eyes had not deceived me. Nor had my ears. Hannah and Petr — here, after all!

I took stock of what I had seen. The fence had been an ordinary fence. A waist-high, simple timber fence with a small gate without a lock. No sign of guards either.

An ordinary garden. Grass, withering in the heat. A few small trees, fruit trees. A kitchen garden with onions and lettuce, and stuff I hadn't had time to identify.

I'd seen a bike. The pool. A basketball hoop on the garage. A chicken coop. No dog, not one I'd heard, at least.

All very ordinary. And why wouldn't it be? What need was there here of guards and security fences. Where were two little foreign kids going to go if they climbed over the fence and made a run for it? How far would they get? The other side of the potato field? Then what?

It was going to be easier than I'd thought.

First, I set off back to the pension, to bring the car closer. After that, I would make it up as I went along. I had the car, money and the kids' passports. I had everything we needed for a sudden and clean break from Zuberec.

★   ★   ★

Wrong. There was one thing I didn't have, but I'll come to that later.

First, buzzing with my amazing discovery, I walked back to the pension and collected the few things I had left there. Then I started the car and eased it quietly along the lanes. I parked about fifty yards away, round a corner and out of the sight line from the house where I had seen the children.

I sat still for a few moments and rehearsed what I wanted to happen. There would be guards somewhere. You didn't take hostages and then leave them totally unguarded, even if they were just kids. If I took things easy, hopefully the guards would stay out of sight, and continue to take their siesta, or whatever.

The kids had nothing essential here with them. Even their backpacks had been left in the hotel in Jetřichovice. So there need be no nonsense about packing a bag, whatever Hannah might think. It would be a straight matter of in and out. With luck, no one should even notice what was happening. We would be out of Zuberec and well down the road before the alarm could be raised.

Alternatively, I was ready to fight if necessary. I didn't have a gun but I had a tyre lever and my fists and feet. More than that, I had surprise on my side. They weren't going to know what hit them.

I was ready.

Let's go!

I got out of the car and didn't slam the door shut. I left it slightly open. The ignition key I left in the lock. I might need any second or two I could win.

Deliberately not hurrying, I sauntered back along the lane between the houses. I willed a suspicious dog behind a fence not to bark. It didn't. I kept going.

Thirty yards now. I could hear Petr's shriek as he hurled himself into the cool water again. Hannah was saying something that sounded like a reprimand. Bossy big sister. I heard no other voices. A passing bee was the next noisy creature.

Ten yards. I reached the corner of the garden and paused behind a small conifer. So far as I could see, there was no one else in the garden. Good . . . so far.

I gave a little whistle. Hannah heard. She slipped off the swing she was using and stood peering around, puzzled. I waited until her eyes had found me before I waved and beckoned.

She stared hard, disbelieving. Then I saw her smile, and she broke into a run.

'Frank . . . '

'Ssh! Get Petr.'

She nodded, grinned happily and turned to run back to the pool. She had a quiet word with Petr, who promptly clambered out of the pool and came racing across the lawn, water streaming off him. Hannah followed, also at a gallop.

I had them both. We could go.

Wrong. The one thing I didn't have was the kids' agreement.

30

'What are you doing here, Frank?' Petr giggled.

'I came to get you, to take you home. Come on! Let me lift you over the fence.'

Petr laughed aloud.

Hannah stepped back. She looked puzzled.

'Hannah!' I hissed. 'Come on. Hurry! The guards will be back soon.'

'What do you mean?' she asked. 'I don't understand.'

'We're going home,' I said again. 'Now, come on!'

They both stood still and stared at me as if I wasn't right in the head. This was proving more difficult than I'd expected. Had they lost their facility with English in such a short time? They were both puzzled, as well as uncooperative.

'Hannah? What's the matter?'

'I don't understand. I thought you must have come to join us here.'

I was beginning to realize something was wrong. 'Here, Hannah? What do you mean?'

'This is our grandmother's house, Frank.

Our other grandmother. Mum said we were to be in Zuberec all summer. It's wonderful here.'

It was my turn to stare with disbelief.

'Your mother knows you're here?'

'Of course. She said we will be safe with Grandmother. So we wait here for her.'

Of course. Vlasta. My spirits sank. What an absolute bloody fuck-up!

'I'll get Babička,' Petr said.

He was off running before I had the wit or the will to say no.

★ ★ ★

I took out my phone. 'Hannah, would you like to speak to your mother?'

'Maybe,' she said, smiling. 'But, Frank, I have my own phone, and we speak to her every day anyway.'

Bloody Vlasta!

I switched my phone off and turned away. 'OK, Hannah. I understand now. It was good to see you both again.'

'Wait, Frank! You must meet my grandmother.'

I could see a bulky, black-garbed woman coming across the lawn with Petr. My heart sank even lower. But what alternative did I have? She might have called the police if I'd run away, and accused me of attempted child abduction.

She was actually very pleasant. She smiled and, with Hannah interpreting, said it was an honour for her to meet someone from England. It was particularly wonderful — amazing even! — that the children had met someone visiting Zuberec who they knew. She was so pleased. I must come into the house and have tea with them.

I didn't. I said something about how I was on holiday, had just arrived and must return to the pension. But it wasn't enough. I had to have a cup of black tea. Then I left.

That was enough humiliation for one day.

★   ★   ★

All the way home I practised what I would say to Vlasta. In the car, on the road to Bratislava, I did it. I did it again at the airport, and on the plane. Then on the drive back from Newcastle I had run out of things to say, and names to call her. I was numb by then.

One thing I knew now was how Harry George had become acquainted with gangsters from Slovakia. Vlasta hadn't just been the interpreter. She had been right there in the middle of it, the facilitator. Her ex-husband, or ex-partner or whatever he was, had been just the right man for Harry to meet when the business needed an injection of capital. How was Harry to know things would get out of hand?

No mystery at all now about their meeting. Apart from the question of how I could have been so gullible. The answer to that, I suppose, was that Vlasta was a tough and wily woman at the peak of her powers. She had certainly fooled me.

She wasn't home when I got back to Risky Point. I went over to see Jimmy, who was still mending the lobster pots that rarely saw the sea these days. As he said, it was easier to get lobster from Iceland or Tesco, if you really wanted it. It didn't hurt your back so much.

'Hi Jimmy. How you doing?'

'About the same,' he said judiciously. 'Been far this time, Frank?'

I shook my head. 'Anything happen while I was away?'

'Not much. That little dark-haired fellow in the leather jacket came back and talked to Vlasta one time. There wasn't any trouble.'

I smiled. I was relaxed now. Sandor was probably looking for dancers for his new club, hoping to persuade the mother of his children to get her kit off once again. Help him become even richer. She would be good at that even now. She had all the talent needed.

'You look tired,' Jimmy said sympathetically.

'Me? Well, what do you expect? I'm getting too old for this game. I don't understand things so good any more.'

Jimmy chuckled. 'I told you she was trouble,' he said. 'The first time I laid eyes on her. I told you that before she got out of the car.'

I swore at him and turned to go back to the house.

'She said she won't be long,' he called after me. 'She had to go for some coffee.'

I nodded and kept going. Vlasta, the housewife, eh? As well as everything else she was.

★ ★ ★

I didn't waste any more time when she returned. 'You didn't tell me Sandor was the children's father,' I said.

The welcome-home smile disappeared. She stopped herself giving me a kiss. She stood still. Then she turned and put the jar of coffee down on the kitchen table. At least she hadn't lied to Jimmy about that.

'Where have you been, Frank?'

'Zuberec.'

'Oh?'

I hoped the shock I was giving her was as great as the one I'd received in Zuberec. She deserved it. She deserved worse. I felt thoroughly evil. She had made me like this, with her lying and her deceit.

'OK,' she said. 'Now I will tell you everything. No more evasions.'

'Would be nice.'

She didn't seem to notice my sarcasm. No doubt she was busy concocting a new web of lies and deception. I relaxed. I was composed. I had the upper hand at last. Vlasta was struggling.

'Sandor is not my children's father.'

'I've been to Zuberec, Vlasta.'

'You met Gisella?'

'The grandmother?'

She nodded.

'Yes, I met her. She was very pleasant. Gave me a cup of tea, with a slice of lemon in it. I wouldn't have guessed she had a son like Sandor.'

'Sandor is not her son.'

'No?'

She shook head. 'The children's father, Marek, my first husband, is her son. He also is from Zuberec.'

'Just like Sandor?'

'Yes. Exactly.'

I sighed wearily. 'You're trying too hard, Vlasta. Why not give it up, this pretence, this fantasy?'

She said nothing for a few moments. Then I noticed her shoulders quivering. 'Come on, Vlasta,' I said impatiently. 'For once in your life stop acting, for God's sake!'

She turned then and threw herself at me, fists flying, feet kicking, tears streaming. 'You don't believe me!' she screamed. 'Everything I tell you is true, and you don't believe me.'

We wrestled a bit. She calmed down. The sobbing continued. I began to feel rotten. I sat her down on the sofa. Dried her eyes with a tissue.

'OK, Vlasta,' I said with a sigh. 'Tell me.'

'It is like I said,' she said sorrowfully. 'But it is not what you think.'

'It never is what I think, Vlasta. It hasn't been from the beginning. I thought I was signing up for a simple driving job, not deep immersion in the gangland culture of most of Europe.'

31

It was hard to stay mad at Vlasta for long. Hard for me, that is. I didn't know about the likes of Harry George and friend Sandor, not to mention the late, unlamented Leroy.

'Just tell me,' I urged. 'Don't try to sweeten the pill. Just tell me what's going on. And make it the truth this time.'

'Sandor and my first husband, Marek, both grew up in Zuberec. I knew them both because my family went there in summer for holidays, and we are all the same age.'

Nice cosy little world, I was thinking. Who would have thought that one of them would grow up to be a stripper and another a gangster?

'One year ago Sandor approached me. I had not heard of him for many years, not since I stopped going to Zuberec when my husband and I parted. But he had somehow heard of my re-marriage, and he knew who I was now married to. These people,' she added, 'they know such things — don't ask me how.'

I nodded. It was true. There was probably a website where international gangsters and criminals of all persuasions could keep up to date on their colleagues and rivals. It made sense. Maybe they had an annual conference, too, like other business leaders, a chance to catch up on all the news.

'So Sandor knew you were married to Harry George, and he knew what you were — had been, that is — and he knew what Harry was?'

'Of course. That is why he contacted me.'

How very sensible. They all were. Such sensible, rational people. You couldn't fault them for that.

'What did he want?'

'At first he said he wanted me to introduce him to Harry. They had mutual business interests, he said, and needed to talk.'

'Then what?'

'I did not want to do that. I know Sandor, what he is like. He was always trouble. So I said no.'

'And?'

'In the end I had no choice. Sandor kept pressing me. Eventually, he said unless I cooperated my children would have a smaller family, fewer relatives. He would start killing, and go on until I cooperated.'

'Their father? Their grandmother?'

She shrugged. 'Who knows? But I believed him. I have always known what he is like.

'So I told Harry. He was interested. They talked on the phone. Then they met, several times. I don't know exactly what was said, but Sandor was interested in buying into Harry's business, I think.

'The business was not doing so well. Harry needed money, so he agreed. After a while, Sandor was lending him money or buying a share of the business — I don't know.'

All pretty much as I had understood. Neat and tidy. Mutual interests and needs coming together. The gangsters' world.

'What did you think?'

'I had wanted to leave Harry for a long time, but I couldn't. I had no money, no nothing. Then one day I had a chance. I learned that Harry would pay Sandor some money, a lot of cash in sterling. It was the annual settlement. Yes? Perhaps the repayment of a loan. I knew about it, and I knew where the money was kept.'

She shrugged and added, 'So I took it. I knew Harry would be in trouble then. I hoped he would have no time to think about me. I hoped Sandor would also be too busy. It would be his chance to take over the business, with Harry defaulting on the loan. So I took the money and ran, with the children.'

And I was the mug she ran to, and who she

involved in something that was nothing to do with me. Great plan.

But she had paid a terrible price already, with the murder of her parents and the abduction of her children. It would have been better for her to have run without the money, but then she wouldn't have had the wherewithal. Such terrible choices she had faced.

Then I realized she was at it again. She couldn't help herself: the children!

I tut-tutted. 'Vlasta! You're not very good at lying, but you keep on doing it, don't you?'

She looked at me, all wide-eyed and innocent. 'I have told you the truth!' she protested.

'Only some of it, Vlasta.'

'What is wrong?'

The children were at their grandmother's home, but Vlasta hadn't spirited them away and got them there herself.

'You reached an agreement with Sandor, didn't you? Sandor wanted Harry's business. You wanted to leave Harry and have money.

'So it was probably agreed that in return for setting everything up, you could take and keep some of Harry's money. That would give you what you wanted. It would also give Sandor what he wanted, because if Harry couldn't pay, Sandor would be entitled to take over the business. And that was what he wanted. Right?'

She sulked for a moment or two. Then she reluctantly agreed. 'It is like I said,' she insisted. Then, when she saw my face, she added, 'Nearly like I said.'

But she and Sandor had both reneged on the deal. Like Vlasta, Sandor wanted *all* the money. Harry's business wasn't enough.

★   ★   ★

The complications started when Bill Peart phoned that evening.

'Glad to find you at home for once.'

'Oh, you know me, Bill. I'm never far away.'

'Not for long anyway.'

'Not for long,' I agreed. 'I'm far too busy.'

'Busy!' He snorted and somehow stopped himself launching into a tirade about what being busy really meant.

'Frank, I thought I'd let you know things are moving fast.'

That put me on full alert. 'What's happening, Bill?'

'We're moving in on the Harry George empire in a few hours. The club, the industrial premises, the properties — everything. We've got a court order. We're ready to go. Anything you want to tell me?'

It was good of him to tell me this. But it was a leak, all the same. He could find himself in trouble over this. He needed a quid pro quo from me, just in case.

'The business has a new de facto owner, Bill. Guy called Sandor. I don't know his surname. He's a Slovak.

'He bought and muscled his way in, and may have ordered Harry's murder. I'm not sure about that. Anyway, he's putting pressure on Harry's widow, Vlasta, to sign everything over to him legally.'

It was a leap. I briefly wondered if a legal documentary transfer of ownership could make an illegal business legal. It would take better brains than mine to work that one out.

'He's a what?' Bill said. 'Run that past me again.'

'A Slovak — someone from Slovakia.'

'Is that a country?'

'It is now, yes. It's next to the Czech Republic.'

'One of them places.'

'One of them,' I agreed.

'That's the East European connection, then. And he thinks he's getting Harry's business? He's in for a shock. Anything else you can tell me?'

I hesitated but decided not to tell him any

details of the pressure being put on Vlasta. He had enough on his plate without having to worry about the safety of foreign nationals in a far-away country. Time was pressing.

'Later,' I told him. 'There's some other stuff I'll give you later. Good luck.'

★   ★   ★

That was one complication. Another was one that had just occurred to me. Why was Sandor still putting pressure on Vlasta? She had done what she had said she would do, and had said she would sign the transfer document when it came. It didn't make sense, unless there was still something I didn't know about.

'Vlasta, you're doing what Sandor wants. So why is he making threats now?'

She shrugged and looked away.

I sighed wearily. 'You've got to stop this lying, Vlasta. Your nose is going to grow so big you'll not be able to see anything else.'

She looked briefly alarmed by that prospect. Then she shook her head. 'I don't know why,' she said dispiritedly.

But I thought I could guess.

'It's the money, isn't it? Were you supposed to give it to Sandor, not keep it?'

Talk about getting blood out of stone!

There was much head shaking and muttering before she finally said with no little defiance, 'I could keep some of it. We agreed!'

Some of it. It was my turn to shake my head now. The woman was amazing. I was impressed by her sheer effrontery.

'Some of it, Vlasta. But you took and kept it all.'

'I gave you some,' she pointed out, trying to give me something to worry about.

'And,' I said firmly, 'the man wants it back, because it's his money, money Harry owed him.'

Her sulky silence told me I was right on the button.

'Anyway,' she added, 'I don't have it now. I don't have any of it.'

'But Sandor thinks you have?'

'Maybe. But I have no idea where it is. You gave it to Harry and Leroy, you said.'

That was true. At last!

At last we were getting somewhere. At long last, I felt I knew most of what had been going on. But it was a long way from being over. I knew that.

32

So even though she was loath to admit it, Vlasta had done a deal with Sandor. They, too, had mutual interests. Vlasta took the money that Harry was due to pay back to Sandor. That put Harry in serious trouble. It also put Sandor in control, and gave Vlasta the chance to escape with the children to a new life.

So far, so good. Except Vlasta had been the first to renege on the deal. She had hung on to all the money, instead of keeping her share and handing the rest over to Sandor. Game on!

Sandor had persuaded Leroy to change sides, and must have commissioned him to take out Harry, as well as recover the money.

But Leroy had also reneged on whatever his deal with Sandor was, and gone for broke. He had kept all the money, just as Vlasta had tried to do before him. And he must have thought he was safe until I caught up with him.

Honour among thieves? Not much.

★ ★ ★

What now? Well, Sandor still wanted the money, but didn't know where it was. I was the only one who knew that.

Sandor did have de facto control of the business — for a few hours, at least. Until Bill Peart took over. After that, Revenue and Customs might well claim it, for all I knew.

Sandor also had the children. He must have arranged with Vlasta to have his guys take them and lodge them back in Zuberec. They would be safe there, with their grandmother. That suited Vlasta well enough, but also gave Sandor a hold over her. She knew what would happen if she refused to sign over Harry's business when the time came.

It was certainly a tangled web that had been woven. But it was about to become a lot less tangled. Soon there wouldn't be a business for anyone to claim or own. Then what?

★ ★ ★

We found out the next morning, when Sandor phoned Vlasta and they had a short, one-sided conversation in whatever language it was they preferred to use with each other.

Afterwards, Vlasta turned to me and said, 'Sandor.'

I nodded, and waited.

'He says the police have moved in and taken over Harry's properties. There is nothing he can do right now.' She shrugged. 'He is leaving, before they catch up with him, too.'

'So what does he want? Why did he ring?'

'He says he wants his money back — all of it.'

'The million pounds?'

'Yes.'

'That's reasonable. But you told him you don't have it?'

'Yes.'

'And?'

'He doesn't believe me, or doesn't care what the truth is. He thinks I can get money anyway.'

We were down to basics now.

'And if you don't find the money?'

'He will have the children killed, and their grandmother. Then he will kill the children's father. After that, he will kill me.'

I nodded. No surprises there.

'Sandor must have an awfully big grudge against you.'

'It is true.' She nodded. 'It is because I would never have sex with him when we were young. I always preferred Marek.'

There wasn't much to say to that. Vlasta,

woman of the world, knew exactly what she had got herself into. So did I now.

★ ★ ★

Sandor had set a time limit: two days. He would wait and watch for two days. Then he would start. When I looked outside, I saw the watching and waiting had already begun. A big, black SUV stood at the entrance to the track.

There was a lot to think about.

'Presumably, you don't have access to a million pounds?' I asked rather forlornly.

She shook her head and looked at me as if I was stupid. 'What do you think?'

Sandor might take an IOU, I thought, but I doubted it. He wanted his money now. Then he would get out and go home. Maybe. Sex with Vlasta might still be on his to-do list.

I could see only one way for us to get out of this. I would have to negotiate, and promise him good things to come.

★ ★ ★

'Can you phone Sandor?'

She tried and shook her head. 'Only his answerphone.'

251

So I needed to go and see who was in the big, black SUV parked along the track.

Two men. They watched me approach on foot. One lowered a window as I reached the vehicle.

I nodded to him. 'I want to speak to your boss. Can you contact him for me?'

He just stared hard at me.

'Sandor,' I said. 'I want to speak to him.'

He was still impassive. So I began to mime what I wanted. High-stakes charades.

'I heard you,' he said after watching this for a while. 'I know what you want.'

'So? Are you going to do it?'

'What do you want to talk to Sandor for?'

I smiled and said, 'Get him. He'll want to talk to me.'

'I don't think so. The time for talking is over.'

I took out my phone and began pressing numbers. Then I held it up for him to see the screen.

'That's 999. The emergency number. OK? I'm going to press call. When they answer, I'm going to tell the police two murderers employed by Harry George or a Slovak called Sandor have staked out my house. My guess is they'll be here in a couple of minutes. So what do you want to do?'

He got out his mobile and made the call.

There was a brief exchange. Then he handed the phone to me.

'Sandor?'

'What do you want?'

'Frank Doy here. I — '

'I know that. What do you want?'

'We should meet.'

'Why?'

'I'm working for Vlasta. I need to convince you that she doesn't have the money you want, and can't possibly lay her hands on it. She simply doesn't have much money at all.'

'She knows what the outcome will be, in that case,' he said crisply.

'But I might be able to help you.'

'I've seen your house, Doy, and your car. I've checked out your business. Cut the crap.'

Time to get real.

'OK. I don't have quite that much money. Even if I had, I wouldn't give it to Vlasta to give to you. What I do have is information.'

'Keep talking.'

'I know where Leroy went with the money. And I know where he is now. Think about it, and phone me back on my own phone if you want to talk.'

I switched the phone off and handed it back to the guy behind the wheel.

'Cheap phone, that,' I said, unable to help

myself. 'If I were you, I would look for something better.'

I didn't bother waiting for his reply as I turned and set off back to the cottage.

★ ★ ★

'What now?' Vlasta said.

'We wait.'

'He's going to call you back?'

'I think so.'

'What did you tell him?'

'I told him I know where Leroy is. He'll want to talk about that.'

She snorted with disdain, and disbelief. 'You told him that? Now he'll kill you, as well!'

'I really don't think so. He'll think that where Leroy is must be where the money is.'

Still she shook her head.

'And he would be right,' I added softly.

That brought her head up and round. 'Frank!' she said, rushing to throw her arms around me, for all the world as if I were the most important person in her life. 'You are so wonderful.'

33

'I'm not talking on the phone,' Sandor said.

That was a pity. But not unexpected.

'But you do want to talk?'

'I'll send a car.'

'It will go back empty. Where do you want to meet? *Aphrodite's?*'

He ignored that little provocation, which told me the conversation mattered to him.

'How about the seafront?' I suggested. 'Redcar?'

'The railway station. Eight this evening.'

The phone went dead. I shrugged and glanced at my watch. I had plenty of time.

Vlasta was looking expectant. 'We're meeting,' I told her. 'This evening.'

'What time are we — ?'

'Not you, Vlasta. I'm meeting him. Alone.'

I thought she was going to argue, but she nodded and said, 'Perhaps that is best.'

I moderated my position. 'You come into Redcar with me, if you like, but not to the meeting place. I don't want to risk him grabbing you.'

'I will stay here,' she said briskly. 'You go alone, Frank.'

So I did. I drove into Redcar, mentally rehearsing what I was going to say. It had to be good. There could be no mistakes now. The lives of Hannah and Petr were at stake, not to mention those of the rest of us.

I made a point of getting there exactly at eight. I wanted my punctuality to stick in his mind. It might be important, given the plan I was working on.

I recognized his car in the parking area, the big Audi. There was no one in it. The station was pretty well empty, too. A train came through every half hour or so, if that, in the evening. As a venue, it wasn't bad.

I saw Sandor and another man at the far end of the platform and began walking towards them. No doubt there would be someone else at the opposite end of the platform. Men like Sandor didn't survive long if they were careless enough not to watch their back.

I stopped a few yards short and let him come to me. The other guy moved in front of Sandor. I stood still and let him run his hands around me quickly and efficiently.

'What have you got for me?' Sandor asked when his man moved back behind him.

'Leroy went to Greece when he left you. A

Greek island — Rhodes. Harry had a house there. That's where the money is.'

There was a brief flicker of surprise across his face. 'Where is this house?' he asked.

I shook my head. 'I'm not going to tell you immediately. I suggest we go there, separately, for safety reasons. At the same time, Vlasta will go to Zuberec to collect the children. When she phones and tells me they are safe, and she is safe, I will take you to the villa where Leroy is.

'That's the deal. I get Vlasta and the kids; you get Leroy and the money.'

He shook his head. 'Who the fuck do you think you are, Doy?' he said, bristling. 'You think I'm going to listen to crap like that? Go halfway round the world? Me?'

'That's the deal,' I repeated. 'Think about it.'

I stared at him a long moment. Then I turned and walked away. At the far end of the platform I saw a figure approaching, waiting for a signal from Sandor.

I stopped and turned back round. 'Anything happens to me, Sandor,' I warned, 'you don't get to find the villa. Also, my cop friends are keeping an eye on me. I'm fireproof while I'm here. So is Vlasta.

'We both go to Rhodes, you get Leroy and you get your money back. Vlasta and the kids go free. I come home. That's it. Finished. End of story.'

Then I got out of there. Let him think it over. I was tense but I believed he would go for it. The advantages would all be with him once we moved offshore. He would be able to see that.

Just in case, though, I would have a Plan B.

* * *

Vlasta looked at me expectantly when I got home. I shrugged. 'I think he'll buy it, but I have to wait for him to let me know.'

She accepted that and disappeared. I let her go. I needed to do some thinking.

But I didn't do much. The tension was too great. Instead, my eyes followed the minute hand dragging its weary way round the clock face. If the call didn't come within an hour my bet was it wouldn't come at all. That's when I would need Plan B, which, so far, I didn't have.

At five minutes to the hour the phone rang. I picked it up.

'OK,' he said. 'We'll do it your way.'

I could breathe again.

34

The airport in Rhodes looked just the same as on my last visit. Hot, dry, white, dusty. To me, unpleasant.

But I felt good. I was running something I understood at last.

Somehow I had persuaded Vlasta she wasn't coming with me. Her role was to go to Zuberec, collect the children and disappear to somewhere far from there. Only when I heard from her would I meet Sandor. Yes, I had assured her: I will protect myself I promise.

I got to Rhodes early. There were plans to make before I hired a car and drove to Pefkos. And there were things to do once I got there.

★   ★   ★

No one had been inside the villa since I left. The tell-tales I had put in place told me that. No one had stepped inside either of the doors and no one had disturbed the windows. I was satisfied.

The place was clean, too. I had half

expected to find a certain smell lingering but my cleansing operation must have been more thorough than I had feared. All the same, the kitchen wasn't a place where I would ever want to eat.

There wasn't a lot to do before Sandor arrived. I fashioned a rough timber cross with Leroy's name on it, which I stuck into the ground as appropriate. Then I examined the several handguns Leroy's bag held and tucked them away. After that, I was done, my preparations made. So I left and moved across to the nearby restaurant where I had rented a room again. Then I waited for Vlasta to call.

★　★　★

The call came the next morning, just before eleven.

'Frank?'

'Hello, Vlasta.'

'I've got them, Frank. We're all OK.'

I closed my eyes with relief.

'Where are you now?'

'About to cross the border, back into the Czech Republic. I picked up a car in Bratislava. Now we're going to Prague. I have friends there.'

'What sort of friends, Vlasta? You can't

afford to contact anyone from your old life. Sandor may be able to find you if you do.'

She chuckled. 'Don't worry! These are really old friends, from before I became an exotic dancer.'

'That's good. Keep to that, Vlasta. Don't go anywhere near people and places Harry and Sandor might know about.'

'All right. I understand. What will you do now, Frank?'

'What I said. I'll call you later, when it's all over.'

'Take care, Frank. Remember, we love you!'

Oh, yeah.

Still, I smiled. Perhaps they did.

★　★　★

I could go to work now. There was no hurry but I had to keep my word to Sandor. If I didn't, he might not keep his to me.

Oh, yeah! Fairy tales are such fun.

I phoned him. He was at a hotel near the airport.

'Where are you, Frank?'

I ignored the question and gave him the address of the villa. 'I'll be there about seven this evening, Sandor. I'll expect you when I see you. That OK?'

'Sure, Frank. I'll be there.'

He sounded genial. He should be. Things were working out nicely for him.

I left it up to him whether he waited inside or outside the villa. But I was pretty sure he would be there well before me, eager to tear Leroy limb from limb. He probably imagined he wouldn't need me now. He could do what he wanted to do with Leroy, pick up the money and get out long before I arrived.

I hoped that was what he did think.

★   ★   ★

I approached the villa with some trepidation that evening. I didn't expect Sandor to keep to our bargain, but at least he wouldn't kill me till he found the money. I hoped.

I walked to the villa. I walked through the day's dust, through the fragrant sage and wild mint, through the cooling air in the shadow of the mountain. I walked up the long drive from the main road in full view. I wanted them to see me coming, if they were there.

It was warm still. Insects filled the air. I was sweating heavily. My shoes kicked up clouds of white dust. A goat stopped grazing on a shrub without leaves to stare at me. I wiped my forehead with the back of my hand and fingered the sweat and grit out of my eyes.

Then I pressed on. My heart rate rose as I neared the gate.

The gate was open. I paused before going through. Took a last look round. This was it. I didn't have to go any further. I could still back off, and make a run for it. Let them do their worst. I was tempted. Vlasta and the kids were out of it now. So why not?

I went through the open gate. Vlasta might believe they were out of it, but Sandor could find them. I knew that. It might take time but he would find them. Somebody would. All it would take was money. Wherever in the world they were, he would find them.

As I approached the house I heard the soft shuffle of feet behind me. I kept going. Too late now to back out. I had to see it through.

In the fading light, another figure came down the front steps towards me. Two, then. I wondered if there were more. How many? Perhaps one more, a car load, my guess.

Where was the other one?

I stopped and stood still. I let the guy coming down the steps reach me and pat me down for weapons.

'Nothing?' he queried with a chuckle.

'Nothing,' I agreed.

'You make it easy,' he said, still chuckling.

'It's how I work.'

He motioned me to go ahead. I climbed the steps.

The fourth guy was inside the house, with Sandor. He stood like a family retainer, alert to his patron's every wish, except he held a gun by his side. Already, I thought with a sick feeling. This was not going to go well.

'He's clean,' the man who had frisked me said.

Sandor nodded. He looked at me grim-faced. 'You're a fool,' he snapped.

He was right. I knew that.

'We found Leroy,' he said.

'You did?'

'And we left the hole in the ground open.'

I shrugged. I knew then it was hopeless. We really didn't have a deal.

'Mind if I sit down?' I said with a sigh, moving towards the kitchen table. 'It's so hot. I'm tired.'

The guy behind Sandor raised his gun. I ignored him and sat down at the table. I put both elbows on the table and rested my head in my hands.

'Where's the money?' Sandor snapped.

'Vlasta is away from Zuberec,' I said, leaning back in my chair. 'You going to stick to our agreement? You going to leave her alone? Her and the kids?'

'Where were you, pal, when they were

264

serving out brains? In the can?' Sandor bristled with contempt. 'Where did Leroy put it? Do you know?'

I placed both hands flat on the table and leaned backwards slightly, tilting the chair. 'You going to keep the bargain, Sandor?'

I balanced the chair on its back legs, now just using my fingers, my thumbs under the edge of the table top.

'You kill Leroy yourself?'

I nodded.

Sandor looked interested. 'He was a tough guy.'

I nodded.

'He was pretty badly smashed up.'

'I had no choice.'

'He tell you where the money was?'

'It was here with him. I saw it.'

'Crap!'

'I saw it.'

'I don't believe you. You're full of shit.'

I balanced the chair now with only the fingers of my left hand. I didn't need my right hand for that.

I couldn't feel it. It wasn't there. For a moment I was in danger of panicking. I glanced down at the table and realized it had been moved slightly. My fingers slid sideways an inch or two and I found it.

'The money's not far from here,' I said

slowly. 'Within easy reach. Do we have a deal still?'

Sandor snorted. 'Quit stalling!' he said, raising his voice. 'You want the shit beaten out of you before we shoot you? You're not leaving here alive, Doy. You do know that?'

'What? No deal, Sandor?'

'You're a fool,' he said again. He nodded at the man with the gun. 'Shoot him in the leg first.'

The man raised his weapon. I shot him. Because my hand and gun were under the table, the bullet hit him in the groin. It stopped him. He screamed. His gun hand dropped.

I pulled my hand out from under the table and shot Sandor twice, hitting him in the chest both times. He went down.

I stood up then and shot the gunman again, making sure. Then I turned to the door as it burst open and opened fire, hitting the man who had frisked me.

There was still one left. I paused to finish off Sandor, shooting him in the head. Then I went looking for the last man.

He was clever, staying outside and waiting for me to come to him. Waiting for me to appear in the doorway, light behind me. I couldn't risk it. I couldn't risk him getting away either. If he told his tale in the right place, I would spend the rest of my life looking over my shoulder, not knowing who to look for.

I took Sandor's gun, the one he had never even drawn, and checked it. Then I went out a window at the back of the house and made my way carefully to the main gate. In cover, I waited.

I was prepared to wait nearly forever. The hard work was done. I wasn't going to waste it now.

I didn't have to wait that long. An hour at most. Then the survivor made his run. The car door, five yards away, opened suddenly. The interior light came on. I shot him as he stooped to get in. That was it. Job done.

★   ★   ★

There never had been any real prospect of my deal with Sandor sticking. I had always known that, had even counted on it. Sandor was not that kind of guy. Once he had Leroy and the money, he would have seen no point leaving me alive. Or Vlasta either.

To be honest, I'm not sure I would have wanted him to be still alive either. There would have been no closure. So once he had made his intentions clear, he had made it easy for me.

There had been a brief moment of panic when my fingers couldn't locate the gun I had taped under the table. That was when I had begun to wish I'd stayed standing and reached for the other gun, the one I had secreted in the bedroom. But to get to it, I would have had to persuade Sandor to go upstairs, and that might have been difficult. So the simple plan had worked well.

★ ★ ★

It was properly dark by the time the last of Sandor's men died. I still had a lot to do. The reopened grave was not going to take four more bodies, I realized as soon as I saw it. Nor did I fancy excavating a hole big enough that would. Not by hand. So all four went into the car Sandor had hired. After that, I refilled Leroy's grave.

With a lot of reservations, I dug up the money bag that had been the cause of so much trouble. I knocked as much dust off it as I could and dropped it outside the gate. It had to go with me, risky or not. Vlasta would need money.

Just one thing left to do now. A big thing, but I hoped it would solve a lot of problems.

I drove the car into the garage that was an integral part of the house. Then I stuffed a rag into the petrol tank, waited till it was well soaked and then pulled it half out. A last look round. Then I lit the rag and walked away.

I collected the money bag and set off along the rough track that ran parallel to the road. Even before I had reached the gate, I heard the petrol tank explode. By the time I was a little way along the track, the whole house was in flames. No one was going to have to eat in that kitchen ever again.

★   ★   ★

'The villa burned down?' Vlasta said on the phone, sounding as if the connection was so poor she distrusted it.

'Completely.'

'What a pity!'

'It might be a good thing, Vlasta. I don't think life there would have been good for you and the children.'

'Oh, I don't want to live in Greece any more.'

'No?'

'No. I want to live in our own country. The children do, too.'

I was surprised. 'Really?'

'Yes, Prague.'

'Is there something I don't know, Vlasta?'

She laughed. She sounded delighted. 'Yes,

there is, Frank. We are with Marek, and we will stay with him. Forever,' she added.

Her first husband. The father of Hannah and Petr.

'Is this true, Vlasta?'

'Yes! He loves us, and we love him. We are back together.'

'That's wonderful. Congratulations.'

I had my doubts, but I hoped for the best. Then Hannah and Petr came on to say goodbye, and I dismissed all my doubts. They were so happy I was prepared to believe Vlasta's 'forever' meant the same as mine.

'One final thing, Vlasta. Do you need money for your new life?'

'No, no! Of course not. We are happy now.'

★ ★ ★

Afterwards, I thought it surprising that Vlasta had not been desperate to know what had happened to the million pounds that had stirred up so much trouble. Bill Peart had the answer.

'Fake,' he told me. 'The notes you gave me were rubbish, made in one of Harry George's little industrial establishments.'

'Counterfeit? Forged?'

'Absolutely. We were pleased to find where all that stuff was coming from. Where did you get those notes from, incidentally?'

'Oh, it's a long story. Abroad,' I added when I saw he was not satisfied with that. 'I picked them up in Greece, and wondered.'

Bill nodded and looked grim. 'Let's hope we did enough to save the British economy. But right now let's get down to the beach and cast these rods.'

His information told me what to do with the holdall I had so perilously and dubiously brought back from Rhodes. Vlasta had said she didn't want money, didn't need it. Now I knew why she particularly didn't want *that* money. It was better put into landfill. I couldn't even salvage any for work on my cottage.

At least the up-front payment she had made to me was legal tender. Wasn't it? I checked. No such luck. 'Made in Middlesbrough' might as well have been stamped on it, now Bill Peart had shown me what to look for.

'You know,' Jimmy Mack confided, 'I was wrong about her. Trouble? She was as good as gold. I'm sorry you've let her slip away.'

'Best thing I ever did,' I said gruffly.

I just hoped Marek knew her well enough to cope.

We do hope that you have enjoyed reading this large print book.

Did you know that all of our titles are available for purchase?

We publish a wide range of high quality large print books including:
**Romances, Mysteries, Classics
General Fiction
Non Fiction and Westerns**

Special interest titles available in large print are:
**The Little Oxford Dictionary
Music Book
Song Book
Hymn Book
Service Book**

Also available from us courtesy of Oxford University Press:
**Young Readers' Dictionary
(large print edition)
Young Readers' Thesaurus
(large print edition)**

For further information or a free brochure, please contact us at:
**Ulverscroft Large Print Books Ltd.,
The Green, Bradgate Road, Anstey,
Leicester, LE7 7FU, England.
Tel:** (00 44) 0116 236 4325
Fax: (00 44) 0116 234 0205

Other titles published by
The House of Ulverscroft:

NEVER LOOK BACK

Dan Latus

Living quietly in Northumberland, ex-spook
Jake Ord is awakened early one morning
by a sniper's bullets that only narrowly
miss. It seems his old life has caught up
with him. In the nearby village, MI5 agent
Anna Mason catches his eye — she's on
duty, but she won't reveal why . . . yet.
Then as Jake thwarts an ambush, he
decides he needs help and he summons
Dixie, an ex-colleague and best friend of
his late wife Ellie. Together, with Anna's
help, they unravel an assassination plot
that has political implications and con-
front the man they hold responsible for
Ellie's untimely death.

A FATAL FALL OF SNOW

Joyce Cato

Spending Christmas in a country farm-house, snowed-in and cooking her favourite traditional, seasonal food, seems like a dream come true for travelling cook Jenny Starling. But the Christmas spirit evaporates because of the family she's cooking for: a rebellious teenage daughter and two resentful sons at loggerheads with their arrogant father. And then Jenny finds a corpse with a knife in the chest sitting at the kitchen table, and the farmer accuses her of the deed. She must act quickly and find the real killer — especially since the assigned police officer seems reluctant to be taking on his first murder case.